Runcible Tales

By

Neal Asher

Contents:

Always With You

Blue Holes

Dragon in the Flower

The Gire and the Bibrat

Walking John and Bird

This isn't my earliest collection – The Engineer published by Tanjen has that distinction (now republished as The Engineer Reconditioned by Wildside Press) – but it does contain some of my earliest stories. Here you see the Polity of my books slowly beginning to germinate. The immortal Horace Blegg puts in his enigmatic appearances while Dragon, that giant extra-galactic alien is being equally as enigmatic, people travel by runcible, the prador are out and about in a massive an almost impossible to destroy warship and there other hints of what is to come. I haven't made many changes from the original – just tidied up *some* of the grammar and spelling. For example the dropshaft of my books is here called a gravity chute and apparently then I assumed 'chute' was 'shoot', so I guess I've learned something.

Revisiting these stories has been interesting. They were written (I think) before I wrote the stories *Spatterjay* and *Snairls* from which the book *The Skinner* had its genesis. In that book humans are enslaved to the alien prador by dint of being infected by a virus that makes them physically indestructible and then being 'cored and thralled' – their brains and part of their spinal column removed to be replaced by a control unit. Here they are PU (Personal Unit) slaves – enslaved by a chunk of technology similar to the augmentations in my books and programmed to think the prador where allies while Polity forces were the rebels. There are other wrinkles here that I've lost in the books, like the weapons proscription via runcibles whereby armaments could not be transported from world to world. And the cyborgs ... but they'll be reappearing sometime soon...

I hope you enjoy this little venture into the past of an imagined future!

Neal Asher 3rd August 2017

ALWAYS WITH YOU

Strobe-flash. An arc rod dragged too quickly across a rough surface. Out of it: a man rolling in black crabskin armour. It may have been a lucky shot. Webster did not know. He spun back and hit the wall of the corridor, slid down it, leaving bits of himself stuck to the scarred plastic. The man reappeared. He was a repro – a PU slave. Webster fired and part of the wall by the man disappeared. The last Webster saw of him was of an arm hitting the ceiling then falling to the floor.

What damage?

Fractured pelvis, multiple fractures of your hip-joint, severed artery-

No need to go on. How much longer can you keep me moving?

Another twenty minutes.

Maybe it would be enough, maybe not. The nanomycelium holding him together was good but it could not perform miracles. Admittedly, without it he would have been dead or in shock by now. His right lung had collapsed and there was a fragment of metal lodged next to his spine, but twenty minutes? He tried to stand up.

'Shit!'

Sorry, neural blockers not ready yet. Rest a moment.

Sure.

He slumped back to the floor.

If I only have twenty minutes I'll have to move quickly.

The whisper voice hissed disapproval.

I know, it's necessary though. They must not know what information has been taken.

Your endorphin and adrenaline levels are very high.

Take them higher if that'll keep me going.

You will pay, after.
Better than dying now or the mission failing.
You may die later.
Yeah, so I'm really going to worry about that now.

Webster stood, dropped his assault weapon and drew his flack pistol. His right leg was hanging like a useless pole, but leaning against the wall and getting what use out of it he could, he continued on. Bones grated in his hip and there was a foam of blood around his mouth.

At the end of the corridor was an elliptical irised door ten metres wide. On reaching it he pressed a crystal into a code reader at its side. This was the moment when he found out if eight operatives had expended their lives to any purpose. The door irised open to expose a gravity chute wide enough to hold twenty men, but then it was not meant for men. He stepped out into space and was accelerated upwards without regard for his wounds. He heard things snapping and blood sprayed from the hole in his leg, but there was no pain, the doctor mycelium had seen to that.

Above him, like a giant blank eye, another door irised and he was decelerated before it. Beyond, in a circular chamber, a lens shape revolved with a rattle of armoured legs. He raised his pistol and fired. Behind him the back of the grav chute disintegrated as if under the burn of a thermic lance. Webster kept on firing.

Chitin and black blood shot in every direction as the flack shells exploded. The crablike Prador tried to back away but it had lost four of its ten legs, all from one side. Clinging to the edge of the irised opening Webster continued firing. Carapace opened to expose softly pulsating organs. One shell inside eviscerated the creature and hissing like a kettle it collapsed.

Webster pulled himself from the chute and moved

unsteadily into the control room. The Prador now lay in ruin with its three remaining legs shivering. Its claws and tertiary manipulators were gone, but its palp-eye still followed his movements. Webster paused by it and put two shells at close range into its brain-pan. It ceased to move.

Irrational of you, Webster.

Fich, when I want your opinion I'll ask for it. In the meantime I'm busy.

It was a medical observation. Your action then was dictated by the effects of your injuries.

What price free will? But you're wrong. What if that Prador had cerebral wiring? It could have watched everything I did and reported it.

The doctor mycelium made no further comment and Webster surveyed the alien consoles around him. To his left was the one he required. He staggered to it and rested his hands on its crystalline surface. His vision blurred.

Webster.

'Yes ... yes, what now?'

You were out for thirty seconds.

Webster checked his inner clock. Fich, the nanomycelium AI that was his so very personal doctor, was correct.

'Damn!... Can't you prevent that?'

No, else I would have.

'Right, speak to me then.'

That will not help. Incidentally, you are vocalizing.

'I didn't ask your opinion, and I know I'm speaking. Just tell me things.'

While Webster ran his fingers over the facet controls, calling up a pictographic computer language on the hexagonal screen, Fich told him things.

The reason for your blackout was an endocrine overload

on your neural receptors. It was, in effect, similar to the blackouts severe alcoholics get. It may happen again, though this is less likely now I am making repairs to your liver.*

'What has my liver got to do with endocrine overload?' Webster asked as he manipulated the controls.

It is where, in the end, everything backs up. Endocrine overload is just one result of me being unable to clear poisons from your body fast enough with your liver damaged.

Time for the virus.

Virus?

Yes, it scrambles their security system before attacking what is secured. There is a delay. During that I must remove what I was sent for.

And that is?

Specifications for certain hull metals.

Then you must destroy this place?

Yes ... as well you know.

Webster shook his head then removed an inch cube of crystal from his belt pouch. This he inserted into a hole in the console. As if sinking into mud the cube disappeared. On the display all the pictographs shrank to a single white dot. Quickly Webster manipulated the controls. More pictographs appeared on the screen.

'Got the bastard!'

The cube resurfaced and Webster snatched it up. He moved to another console, slapped over some manual controls, drew his flack pistol, waited until lights came on under each control, then blasted the console to scrap.

Time to be leaving, Fich.

I am always with you.

Balanced on a blue flame like a scalpel the grain-shaped escape pod arced out into void. Behind it the station peeled as the tidal forces, of the dead sun it orbited, took hold of it and with cruel slowness tore it apart. There were no spectacular explosions. The station, which was two kilometres in diameter, just distorted and pulled apart like something rotten. Few of the five hundred Prador and thousand reprogrammed personal unit slaves knew that they'd had a visitor. All they knew was terror and the cold dry taste of vacuum. In the escape pod Webster saw none of them. He lay unconscious on the floor with the small orange light of his underspace beacon blinking in time with the slow labored beat of his heart.

He floated in urine colored amniotic fluid with tubes jammed into his every orifice. Hideous wounds under pale plastic. Outside the tank, with only a pair of dirty toweling shorts protecting him from the chill of the air, an ancient Japanese man sat on the metal floor, his weird eyes intent, unblinking. A door to one side slid open and a woman in a coverall stood silhouetted in the wedge of harsh light.

'How is he?' she asked.

It was not the Japanese who replied.

'He should be dead. He is being kept alive beyond my function while I repair him,' replied the disembodied voice of Fich.

The woman moved further into the room, looked round anxiously as the door slid shut. She was tall, athletic, her hair black and closely cropped, and her face of standard beauty if ever freed from its tension, its nascent hate. She handed the man a paper cup filled with coffee. He took it and sipped, his eyes not straying from the tank.

'Another five hours and we'll have a live one,' he said, the first words he had spoken in three days. He looked at the woman. 'Doesn't that make thee happy?'

Five hours later the woman returned. The Japanese man was gone – from the room, from the station, no one knew how.

With a feeling of mild surprise that he was able to, Webster opened his eyes and stared up at the ceiling lights.

'Well, you're alive,' said the woman from beside his bed.

'Thank you for your concern, Sheil,' said Webster, his voice grating and weak.

She came to you every day while you were in the tank.

Probably looking for a plug to pull, was Webster's silent reply. He smiled at Sheil while she looked at him without any affection.

'Looks like the mission is on,' he said. She frowned. He continued, 'I imagine you're looking forward to working with me rather than against me now?' Sheil walked away without a word.

The planet breaker was a wedge of exotic alloy ten kilometres long. It had a crew of five thousand Prador and ten thousand human PU slaves. It had hyperlight drive and could project particle beams capable of slicing moons in half from a hundred thousand kilometers away. It carried quark torpedoes in the terraton range. In the five solstan years it had been in human space it had depopulated six worlds and accounted for some thirty billion human beings. The Human Polity had nothing that could stand against it. Human technology had not been ship-based, the expansion of the human race across the galaxy being directly attributable to the runcible gates – direct matter transmission between worlds. The human race retreated before it, evacuating world after world as it wove its erratic course through the stars of the Quarrison drift.

'So this is what it is all about,' said Webster as he looked at the small cube of golden metal in the palm of his hand.

'That's it,' said Helstoff. 'Completely reflective to any laser of any spectrum we have. It's superconductive at any temperature so particle beams and APWs just get sucked away. That bloody ship could crack two or three inhabited worlds before we could even raise it above room temperature. Their field technology keeps all our atomics away and it never gets close enough to a station for us to cross swords at any other level. The Mirabar station was sliced apart from seventy thousand kilometers out.'

'They came close at Chocasta didn't they?'

'Yes, there was that. They managed to gate a moonlet at it from hyperlight. It hit as photonic matter. The flash killed everything remaining on Chocasta. Did their work for them. That's the reason we have this breathing space. The ship is laid up off a gas giant in the Chocasta system. Making repairs. Taking on fuel. Whatever. There are no visible signs of damage.'

Webster put the cube down and picked up a vial no bigger than his thumbnail. He inspected the cloudy fluid it contained.

'And this is it,' he said. 'This is what you'll inject into Sheil?'

'Yes.'

Such was I at my inception, Fich told him.

Webster carefully put the vial back down. It seemed a small thing upon which to bet the future of the human race.

'It should have been me,' he said.

'Not possible,' Helstoff told him. 'Not with a Fich III inside you, and you know they cannot be removed.'

That is not true.
Yeah, but I'd like to be alive after.

Webster strolled down the corridor with his thoughts cold and emotionlessly objective. It had been his idea originally, but then the cargo had been a contraterrene device. The idea had been shelved when it was discovered that no such device could get past the scans of the planet breaker. Now there was a new cargo to go aboard. A door slid open in the corridor and Sheil stepped through. And here it is, thought Webster.

'Come for the show?' he asked her.

'Yes, unlike some on this station I will enjoy this.'

Webster made to walk on, but she stopped him with a hand on his chest.

'Why is it necessary for you to come?'

'Here?'

'No, to the ship.'

Webster snorted.

'Do you think I'm there to check up on you?' He did not wait for her to reply. He did not expect her to. 'I'm not. You hate me because I worked for Earth Central against the Separatists. We are both on the same side now.'

'My home world cannot secede from the Polity now.'

No, her home world was spreading out in a pretty asteroidal ring round her home sun, now.

'You hate the Prador more than me,' said Webster. 'It's why you volunteered. Why you were selected. You know our chances of walking away from this are remote to say the least.'

'Why are you going then?'

'My prime mission is to help you get to the metal of the hull. Only physical contact will work. I have a secondary data gathering mission. This is too good an opportunity to miss.'

Sheil nodded and continued working. Webster walked along behind her. Tight assed bitch, he thought.

You want to have intercourse with her.

Get outa here.

The room was filled with monitors and technicians in blue overalls. It was quiet, none of them felt like talking much about what they were going to do. Beyond the shimmer-shield, at one end of the room, the Prador was held immobile in its restraints, but for its stalked eyes, which were whipping from side to side in its agitation. Two more technicians in surgical body suits stood waiting.

'There is no way of anaesthetizing it?' asked Webster.

Helstoff stepped up beside him scratching at his beard.

'We only know enough about their physiology to do this. There are some things we could have tried, but there is a chance they might have killed it, and we only have this one.'

'Let the bastard suffer,' said Sheil.

Webster glanced at her. She was staring at the Prador avidly.

As they watched, Helstoff gave the signal and one of the surgical techs pulled down a vibroblade cutter on the end of a boom. The blade – a flame of dull glass – whined and went into the Prador's carapace. Fans sucked a spume of dust away as the blade moved automatically in a perfect circle. The vibration was muted. The bubbling scream that came from the Prador was not.

When the cutter completed its circle the tech pulled the blade away then inserted a thin trepanning tool through the cut. She worked it around, then levered the circle out.

'Life signs still at optimum,' someone said.

The Prador was still screaming.

'Okay,' said Helstoff, looking into a screen. 'Maria,

expose the secondary cortex.'

Maria used something like a fish slice to shove a quivering bladder to the edge of the hole. She then lowered a surgical laser on its boom, and from it attached a clamp to the bottom of the hole.

'Imaging,' said Helstoff. Webster stepped back and looked at the screen. It showed the circle and the organs within. Lines were being traced round each organ, grids overlaid.

'We're on auto now. Step back Maria, the AI's taking over.'

As Maria stepped back the laser started flickering. Jets of smoke shot from the hole. On the screen Webster saw selected areas of the mess inside being burnt away. Abruptly the Prador stopped screaming.

'It's not in any pain now,' said Sheil with relish.

She is.

And you are one.

'Do you want to come in for a drink then?' It was more of a challenge than a question.

'Yes, why not?'

Webster entered her cabin waiting for some sarcasm from Fich. It was not forthcoming. He slumped down at the end of an airform sofa and watched Sheil as she filled two tumblers with whisky. There was no asking what he wanted to drink. She was not prepared to be that civil.

'They tell me it was your idea in the beginning?'

'Yes, to use the Prador to get something aboard. We tried it with PU slaves but no joy. We lost one of the only two Prador shuttles we've ever captured. The hope is that they'll be prepared to rescue one of their own.'

'Yeah, and it mustn't give the game away. ... This time

we'll be using that last shuttle?'

'Yes.'

She handed him his whisky and sat at the further end of the sofa, her legs curled under her. Webster noted that the zip of her overall was down further than it had been when they had entered the room. He looked at her. She looked back. They drank their whisky. Abruptly she slid from the sofa, stood up, and pulled the zip all the way down to her shaven crotch. As Webster stood she slipped the material from her shoulders, revealing taut breasts over a taut stomach. He stepped forwards and ran his hands up the front of her body to caress her breasts, then slid them round her back as he pulled her to him. She turned her head away.

'Never kiss me. Never. I don't want your affection,' she said. 'I just want you to fuck me.'

Webster did so, gladly. At the back of his mind there was a hint of a feeling of 'I told you so'. He ignored it. He was used to it.

They lay tangled in sheets and dewed with sweat. Webster ran his finger around one erect nipple then traced lines in the sweat on her muscular stomach. The scratches on his back felt about half an inch deep.

Was that for real?

There was no answer.

Come on Fich. It was wet and warm and I know you can't resist probing other bodies. You were in her as well.

She climaxed so violently I had to retreat from her womb. Your machismo is safe. Do you realize she uses no form of contraception?

What?

Don't worry. I dealt with it.

Webster paused in his doodling.

You can do something about those scratches while you're about it.

The soreness faded. Webster sighed. Sheil turned her head to look at him.

'You might have died in the tank,' she said.

'Unlikely, with the tank and Fich.'

'Do you know what condition you were in when they picked you up?'

'Never thought to enquire.'

'Gangrene in your arms and legs. The doctor mycelium was just managing to sustain life with one damaged kidney, a few spoonfuls of liver and a leaky heart.'

'Is it really necessary for me to know this,' said Webster with distaste. He took his hand away.

'You would have died, but for Blegg.'

Webster sat upright, a cold shiver raking his back.

'Horace Blegg, agent Prime Cause?'

Such an unlikely name for one of the immortal arbiters of human destiny

'He sat by your tank for three days. Kept you alive.'

This is true.

Why didn't you tell me before?

Because you would overreact.

'Fucking hell!'

I told you so.

Sheil said, 'It means this mission is important. Survival of the human race important.'

Webster subsided to the sheets, pulled them over him. He suddenly felt cold, very cold. He reached for Sheil and pulled her towards him. Forgetting himself he tried to kiss her. She put her hands between their mouths.

'I only kiss people I love, and I can never love you.'

'The shuttle is at this moment being gated to Ansalep where it is predicted the planet breaker will strike next. The colonies on the moons of Ansalep are already being evacuated.'

'How will the shuttle be accounted for?' asked Sheil.

'Wreckage from a small Prador war craft is being positioned in the Ansalep system its trajectories consonant with the destruction of the craft near the Ansalep station. The shuttle computer is also being programmed to confirm this, and to confirm that the shuttle put down on an asteroid for repairs,' the AI told her.

'You've made those repairs to the shuttle?'

Webster suppressed the urge to tell her not to be so stupid. AIs did not screw up that way, only humans did. Her problem of course was that like any Separatist she distrusted AIs. The issues were complex but came down to the fact that Separatists wanted their worlds seceded from Earth Central authority - no matter what the majority of the population of their planet wanted - with control taken away from the runcible AIs and handed over to them. A few worlds had managed secession, but never for long. Earth Central normally moved back in when the planetary government fragmented and they were on the brink of war, or when the majority finally discovered that life was not as good as when the AIs had control. The AI that was called Earth Central described humans as fast machines working for slow genes. It was generally agreed that human beings could not be trusted with their own destiny.

'This shuttle survived its mother craft in circumstances similar to these fictional circumstances. The onboard computer has been reprogrammed to take this into account. It did set down on an asteroid for repairs after its mother ship was destroyed.'

Webster said, 'Only that was a few light years away and the shuttle never got the chance to launch again.'

'Did the Prador come from that shuttle?'

When the AI remained silent Webster answered, 'No, it was the pilot of a reconnaissance craft we destroyed.'

'How did it survive?'

'It was outside its craft in a space suit when attacked. The attack ship picked it up later, or rather, it towed it to the local station.'

'You are descending into atmosphere,' the AI told them. Webster caught a hint of the vibration just before the restraint fields pressed him back into his seat. Through the front screen of the delta-wing they saw the a tilted volcanic landscape of yellow and gold and muddy brown. Slowly a huge building with giant chimneys swung into view.

'The sulfur extraction plant,' the AI told them.

Webster nodded to himself. The plant was no longer used. Once sulfur had been brought here, purified, and shoved out into space by mass drivers, where it had been used by huge factory stations in a thousand different processes. The factory stations were still there. The sulfur was now gated from the surface of the world, and purified through the runcible gate. This was not the gate they would be using though. There would not be much left of a human passed through such a gate.

The runcible facility was a transparent dome sat in the middle of the yellow hellscape. Only a scattering of technicians was there to greet them, if greeting it could be called. Sheil went first through the entrance tunnel, the Prador came after supported by AG units, guided by Webster who walked along behind holding a control box. They stepped up onto a dais of black glass and stood before the horns of the runcible, the shimmer of the

Skaidon cusp between, like dew-soaked cobwebs. Sheil strode through first – shimmer and gone. Webster send the Prador through next, its saucer shape seeming to melt into the field. He followed, through the shimmer into the five space spoon, flung by the spoon for light years, caught by another spoon. Here the difference between Prador and human technology: the Prador took ship from world to world, humans stepped. The advantage of convenience to humans was a disadvantage in war. What need did they have of ships?

On the other side Webster stepped out into a chamber little different from the one he had exited, even the technicians wore the same overalls. Beyond the dome of transparent material he saw a moonscape. A technician approached, first Sheil, then him.

'I'm to take you to the shuttle,' said the man.

Webster nodded and followed. Even as they were leaving the chamber he looked back and saw the first of the other technicians stepping into the Skaidon cusp. They were amongst the last to leave Ansalep. The technician guiding them would be the last.

'What is your name?' Webster asked him.

'Sabeck.'

'Is there any news on the position of the planet breaker, Sabek?'

'The AI will communicate the information to you once you are aboard the shuttle before I demount it.'

'You're taking the AI away?'

'Yes.' Sabek looked at him. 'All sentient beings will be evacuated.'

Webster never thought otherwise.

The shuttle was shaped like a flower pot resting on its side, not a window nor a sensor protruded from the thick armour plating that covered it. Webster noted the repair patches welded to its underside and the star shaped burn marks spreading from them. It had been hit by a low intensity laser a number of times. As they approached, one third of the shuttle split away and lowered to expose the interior. Sabek brought an AG trolley loaded with equipment over to them, then touched his fingers below his ear as he listened to his implant.

'Your exos and personal units are here, also weaponry. Further briefing will come from the AI. I must leave you now.' He turned to go, then abruptly turned back. 'Smash those fuckers,' he said, and departed.

Webster and Sheil maneuvered the Prador on board and settled it into its huge pilot's couch, then they returned to the trolley. Quickly they stripped then began to buckle on the exoskeletons normally worn by PU slaves. When they came to the personal units, slug-shaped metal canisters the length of a hand, they hesitated.

'You must not connect the personal units until you are in space,' the echoey voice of the AI told them.

'The time delay is still set at two hours after we receive the carrier signal?' asked Sheil.

'Yes, during this period you will be unable to initiate independent action, though you will be aware of everything that occurs. After this period the PU will continue to function but you will be free to complete your mission. The multipurpose assault system will be on-line and disconnected from the PU. Prior to contact with the planet breaker you will be held in alpha coma.'

'How long is that likely to be for?'

'Not long now. The planet breaker is on its way. Estimated arrival in twenty-eight hours. You will be in detector range in twenty-three hours'

Webster quickly set the digital display in the armour over his forearm.

'What about these?' asked Sheil, holding up a glass ring.

'The neck explosives have been de-activated. You may re-activate them by removing them. There is a thirty second delay.'

'Let's go,' said Webster.

They climbed into the shuttle and crammed themselves into the cramped slave compartment behind the Prador cabin. The shuttle closed up and began to shift as they strapped themselves in. The shifting ceased shortly after as the shuttle went inertia-less.

'I am going off-line in four minutes,' said the AI from the shuttle com. 'You may connect the personal units at your discretion.'

Sheil and Webster looked at each other, then with concentrated professionalism began to check over their MPASs. The weapons were multi-barrelled assault rifles with just about every portable destructive capability. A fibre-optic cable hung from the each MPAS, to plug into their exoskeletons where, via a logistics computer, they were finally connected through the neck ring to the PUs. Webster ran a diagnostic and found every system functional. Using the touchplate he took every one of the six setting down to its lowest. At the highest settings the energy and missile packs would have been quickly depleted.

'Twenty eight hours,' said Sheil, as she rested her weapon across her knees. Webster checked his display.

'It'll go quickly enough when we go into coma. All we've got to do is connect up.'

Sheil looked with distaste at the unit she held, then she lifted it to the side of her head.

'See you in twenty eight hours, give or take.'

The PU made a buzzing sound and clamped to the side of her head behind her ear. She grimaced in pain as the bone anchors connected then appeared momentarily bewildered as the induction field came on. Abruptly she slumped into unconsciousness. Webster studied her. He felt slightly ill.

Could you disconnect me from one of those, Fich.
Yes, though there would be some trauma.
If it doesn't automatically disconnect in the designated time I want you to do so.
Very well.

Webster pressed the PU to the side of his head. The bone anchors went in and he swore. It was like some powerful insect clinging there. A loud droning filled his skull. Blackness.

'...life signs optimal, no response.'

Webster realized he was standing beside the brain burnt Prador. He had no memory of getting there. In his hand he held some sort of instrument taken from one of the shuttle's lockers.

'Unit, return to slave bay.'

Webster walked back to the bay, or rather, he was walked back to the bay. It was a horrible feeling. As he strapped himself in the shuttle lurched. He tried to look at the digital display to check the time. He could not move his head.

Twenty-seven hours. They pulled you out of coma to check over the Prador.

Webster tried to ask a question. The buzzing in his head allowed him nothing.

Sheil is still under.

Webster felt a surge of gratitude for the presence of the doctor mycelium – glad it seemed to be anticipating his questions.

I am linked with you at a deeper level than the PU carrier signal. There is no need for you to try so hard to communicate.

Webster's mouth was dry. He was thirsty. The PU responded by allowing him to turn his head and drink from the neck tube. He felt such gratitude to it. The commanders anticipated his every want. He looked forward to his next battle against the rebels, to fighting at the side of the closest allies of Earth Central … the Prador.

You are being indoctrinated at a subliminal level. I will negate the effects.

Webster felt a sudden surge of panic as he realized what he had just been thinking. Fich had hit the spot.

There.

The panic did not go away.

Yes, this will happen to Sheil once she is taken out of coma.

The shuttle lurched again and there was a distant metallic clang. Webster was able to see a picture on one of the screens in front of the motionless Prador. They were being tractored into the planet breaker. Another clang, a delay, the shuttle cracked open and pressures equalized with painful crackling in his ears. Sheil lurched upright beside him. They both stood, attached their weapons to clips positioned diagonally from shoulders to hip across their backs, walked to the Prador and undid the multitude of straps holding it in place. The air hummed with energy and a tractor lifted the Prador out of the shuttle and carried it away into the depths of a huge bay. Sheil and Webster walked out of the shuttle and stood beside it on the frosted metal floor. Huge shapes moved before them. PU slaves flitted here and there on AG units in the shifting machinery – pilot fish in the mouth of a grouper. Webster saw one of them crushed by a monstrous metal wheel rolling along the floor. He was unable to react.

Twenty minutes.

Webster could not feel the fatigue of his motionless body. The PU was pumping him full of endorphins. At one point the suit had jetted liquid food into his mouth and he had nearly choked before the PU instructed him to swallow. He felt the urge to urinate and a catheter was automatically extruded by the suit. It would have been painful without the endorphins.

Ten minutes.

Webster started to walk with Sheil at his side. It seemed to take forever to reach the irised door at the end of the bay. Their PU's halted them, just before a robot like a giant chrome lobster ran them down, then moved them on to the door. They found themselves in a corridor. Another corridor. A drop shaft. A room lined with comatose PU slaves connected by tubes to the walls. They removed their weapons and placed them on a trolley that ground up beside them.

Now.

Webster snatched his and Sheil's weapons back then turned to her. She stood staring blankly at the opposite wall then began to back into the human-shaped niche. As she did this, tubes began to wind out of the walls reaching for plugs scattered all over her exoskeleton. Webster laid the weapons on the floor and pulled her away from the niche. Her only reaction was a look of puzzlement.

What the hell do I do now?

She will not be free for another two minutes.

Webster held onto her and she did nothing but pull against him in the direction of the niche every now and again. He checked the time and when it was up there was still no reaction.

Try shock.

Webster slapped her face, hard. Her head turned aside and a drool of saliva shot from the side of her mouth. He slapped her again.

'Sheil!'

She stared at him like a drunkard. He raised his hand again and she shoved away from him her mouth suddenly gaping in panic. He caught hold of her arm and she fell. On her knees she made a horrible groaning sound then vomited food paste and water.

'Sheil.'

He pulled her to her feet.

'Rebels!' she shouted, and fought against him. He pinned her back against the wall between two niches.

'There are no rebels! The PU was brainwashing you, a subliminal reinforcement. Snap out of it! Remember why we are here.'

'No rebels?' she said ceasing to fight. 'Oh my god....' She rested her head against the front of his exoskeleton. 'It was so strong. So strong.'

'Are you all right now?'

'Nearly, nearly there.'

'Come on, we have to move.'

Webster picked up her MPAS and clicked it in place on her back. At the door to the room he pulled the rings of explosive from his neck and hers and threw them in the general direction of their allocated niches.

'That should confuse things.'

By the time they were in the corridor Sheil was managing to move by herself.

'I have to get to the hull,' she said.

He noted that her face was white and that she was sweating heavily. Was this her reaction to the PU or ...

It is the mycelium. It is ready.

Sheil said, 'I have to touch the exotic hull metal.'

'How long will it take?'

'Three minutes.'

'Okay, we move.'

Webster considered the best way to go just as the neck explosives went off behind them blasting debris out into the corridor. He led the way through the corridors as a chittering alarm started sounding.

'There's a drop shaft just ahead.'

They rounded a corner and were confronted by two PU slaves with hand weapons. The two did nothing for a moment but stare, then abruptly they drew their weapons. Webster depressed the trigger of this MPAS on setting one. It flared once emptying a micro magazine: one thousand explosive projectiles each the size of a pin head. The two PU slaves hit the back of the shaft in fragments. Webster ran forward then skidded to a halt at the lip just as a light above the shaft turned from amber to purple. He caught Sheil and pulled her back.

'Use AG. They've cut the power.'

Into the shaft, AG units humming in their suits. They shot up past each access point. From one there came laser fire just as they passed it.

'Next one.'

They slowed. PU slaves. Webster fired again on setting one, used up the last five magazines. They left the shaft and ran through the human wreckage. Sheil unclipped her weapon and held it before her.

'Shuttle bay ahead.'

'What about your second mission?' asked Sheil with a weak grin.

'I think this one is quite enough.'

They entered the shuttle bay and ran to one side amongst a chaos of machinery. One of the lobster robots shot towards them. Webster hit it with setting two just as Sheil fired. The robot was hit simultaneously by a particle beam and a cutting laser. It juddered to a halt with black smoke pouring from the gaps in its chrome carapace.

'Yes, the catwalk!' said Webster. Sheil ran in the direction indicated just as he fingered to another setting and fired in an arc into the bay. Smoke missiles exploded everywhere. Webster was on the catwalk after Sheil just as part of the bay floor disintegrated under return MPAS fire. They ran along the catwalk then climbed through complex scaffolding. A wall of metal before them. Was this it?

'Ceramal,' said Sheil, and fired at it. Behind them a beam chopped away part of the catwalk and explosive shells stitched the walls. There was confusion and firing from the bay floor. The Prador did not know what instructions to give. Who the enemy was. Webster kept a lookout as Sheil sliced through the ceramal. After a moment he glanced back to see what was taking her so long. Her cut was no longer than a hand.

'It's too thick!' Panicked.

'Use four. The laser reflects.'

Sheil switched to four and a yellowish beam stabbed the smoke. The ceramal glowed – a spreading patch of red, then white.

'Back off!'

She did. Webster shot the patch with explosive pressor shells. The molten sheet blew in to a cavity ten feet across. Beyond lay the glint of gold. They climbed through into null gravity and used their suit's impellers to get quickly from the hole. Into darkness. Suit lights on.

'Here. Do it here.'

Sheil replaced her MPAS on her back and pulled her gauntlets off. She reached out to touch the hull metal. The mycelium in her body was eager. It had been made for this. This was its optimum growth medium. Fibres shot from Sheil's hands as she touched the golden metal. She screamed as her hands melded there like tree roots. Fibres shot from her face, her head was dragged against the metal. She became one with it, stuck there in a cobwebby mass. From the points of contact the fibres spread and the metal lost its sheen. Knobbly growths broke out on the surface here and there as the adapted fungal mycelium spread, fruited, spored, and spread further. Wood rot in exotic metal, only faster, so very much faster. Suddenly the fibres were gone from Sheil's face and hands, which were now bloody.

'Come on!'

Webster grabbed her arm and used his impeller to blast them away, fast, out past the inner ceramal hull that was only armouring round the shuttle bay. Already the hiss of escaping air could be heard from the contact point. Sheil was leaden and unmoving. They fled down through the darkness of the hull cavity. Explosions suddenly flowered all round them. Webster shoved his burden into a mass of struts and wiry insulation then returned fire. Half a kilometer away. Figures. His fire hit the weakened outer hull and it blew. Vacuum sucked the figures out into starlight. Webster grabbed Sheil again, a dead feeling in the pit of his stomach when he saw the holes scorched in her armour and the cooked wounds. She looked wasted. He held onto her anyway. Ahead the tube of an airlock pushed in from the outer hull. Webster put the MPAS on setting five, all the way up to antiphoton beam. He fired into the ship, trigger continually depressed. Purple flash, a tunneling explosion into the ship. Fire and smoke sucked towards the breech in the hull far above. In the wreckage he found the huge saucer of a Prador space suit. He dragged Sheil inside with him, sealed up, laid quiet, listened to the explosions.

Her pulse was weak but still there. At least whatever had hit her had cauterized the wounds. He inspected each one, applied dressing where he could.

What do you think?

Before Fich could answer there was a huge explosion and the suit shifted. Webster shoved himself off and floated to one of the palp eye visors. Starlit space. One of the moons of Ansalep. A chunk of exotic hull metal drifting past, covered in nodular growths. He floated back to Sheil's side.

She will die before we are picked up.

She told me I must never kiss her.

Not even to save her life?

Webster smiled to himself. She might be as mad as hell, but at least she would be alive to be mad. He leaned down and put his mouth over hers, pushed her lips apart with his tongue. From his tongue, his palate, from the soft tissues of his mouth, Fich extended his filamentous body into her and began to repair the damage. Mouth to mouth in the Prador suit they drifted in space, linked as one by the body of another.

From the surface of Ansalep III the ancient Japanese man stared up into space and watched the planet breaker break and the meteor storm of exotic metal. He saw more, perhaps, than any normal watcher might have seen, and he grinned to himself. The grin was short lived though. After a moment he looked in another direction and saw something that made him appear suddenly very tired. He stepped in that direction, and was gone.

ENDS

BLUE HOLES AND BLOODY WATERS

It was the acoustic quality of the presence of a large body of water that made the creature's shriek sound like a gull's, but this was no sea-bird. It had three wings – two that flapped, the remaining one acting as an air rudder – and its body was without recognisable head or tail. Karl lowered the image intensifier he had been handed.

'How does it make that noise? I can see no mouth.'

The driver of the Model T replica looked down at the waves scrolling along underneath as if they might provide a suitable answer.

'Whistles, in the wings,' he eventually said, as if he had wanted to lie but had been unable to find an effective way to do so.

Karl glanced at him speculatively and raised the intensifier to his eyes again. After a moment he had the creature back in view, a perfect image, the chip in the intensifier correcting for focus, vibration, and traverse. Abruptly the creature dropped from the sky and the chameleon lenses of the intensifier whirred as they followed it down. It went into the sea like a cormorant and the lenses whirred back to centre. How does it feed? Karl wondered, but did not bother to ask.

A cratered blimp of a moon was rising into the indigo sky by the time the peninsula came into sight. Karl noted white water far from the beach and wondered if there were corals or an equivalent here. Much as marine biology was his subject there was only so much one man could study. He knew very little about the seas of 'Arrived' and looked forward to learning a little at least.

'There's the house,' said the driver, whose name Karl had not bothered to discover. He raised the intensifier to get his first look at Jarrol's home. After a moment he decided the driver was wrong. This was not a house, it was a *residence*, but then Jarrol had always been extremely rich. Who else but one with huge amounts of credit could indulge in the pastimes he indulged in?

    The Model T antigravity car came down on the roofport of a structure sprawled across a terrain of rock, jungle, and blue holes. Plants like heather trees and giant groundsels grew in abundance, tangled together by something similar to bramble, but sprouting huge unlikely marrow fruits. Karl saw more of the fliers flitting between the trees and with a blurring of eye might have mistaken them for fruit bats. As the AGC settled down on its ersatz rubber tyres he caught sight of a mantislike creature snatching one of the fliers from the air, then the door clicked open and Jarrol and his spouse Celia were walking across the plasticrete to greet him.

    'Karl! So glad you could make it!'

    Jarrol was as effusive as ever, but Karl detected a note of falsity that had not been there before, or had it? As he stepped out of the AGC he felt a momentary qualm at forcing himself upon his friends like this, but it soon passed. Once out of the blast of the air conditioning he immediately broke out into a sweat. It was hot and humid yet the thirty hours of daylight had nearly ended, and the twenty hour night nearly begun.

    'Good to see you,' he said while Jarrol pumped his hand, and it was. Seeing Jarrol standing before him wearing nothing but monofilament shorts on his tanned and stocky body reminded Karl of his youth, of that irresponsible time seemingly etched in sunlight, when transitory pleasures had been enough, and the galaxy theirs to possess.

    'Reminds me of the T II on the Med,' he said.

'Ah, the Titanic II, what a name for a boat. What arrogance!' He slapped Karl's shoulder. 'Those were the days.'

Karl turned to Celia.

'Celia,' he said, holding his hand out, a smile on his face. He did not say, 'I was hoping you'd be gone by now you conniving slut.'

Celia ignored his hand, came close, and pressed herself against him. She wore a monokini that could probably have been crushed into a thimble. Karl could feel her nipples through his shirt. As she kissed him where his jaw met his neck and as she thrust her pubis against his leg.

'So nice to see you again, Karl,' she said, stepping back. She looked flushed. Perhaps it was the heat.

Karl turned and reached into the AGC to retrieve his travel bag and incidentally hide whatever expression he wore. She was doing it again. After four years she was doing it again, and again he would have to grit his teeth and remember that Jarrol was his friend. At that moment the driver came round the car and spoke quickly, before the greeting continued.

'I'm going to the pool now,' he said, and it sounded defensive.

'Yes, you do that, David,' said Celia, then glanced at Jarrol as if afraid of how he might react.

Karl slung his case over his shoulder and studied her. Dislike? Contempt? What was it he had detected in her voice? The one called David turned to one side with his fingers pressed against his chin in a pose Karl could only view as camp, then he walked away. Conversation stalled for a moment.

'You have a pool then?' Karl asked as they walked from the roofport. Jarrol was all enthusiasm again.

'Oh yes, fifty metres at its widest point and ten metres at its deepest. It's connected into the cave system below the blue holes. Biggest system you've ever seen.'

Karl smiled.

'You still dive?'

'No.. not now.' Jarrol rubbed his hands together in a gesture Karl had not seen from him before. 'No.... Do you still do that unaug' swimming?'

Karl shook his head.

'Not at competition level any more. Too many blurred lines. What is an augmentation?' He shrugged. 'When I started it was booster implants and drugs they were clamping down on. Now ... it's too confusing. Is concentrated muscle growth augmentation, when the same effect can be achieved with heavy exercise and a high protein diet?'

'What I always said,' said Jarrol. 'Never could understand why you went in for it.'

'Because he's stubborn,' said Celia.

Jarrol laughed and Karl laughed as well. He had to admit she was probably right.

They reached stairs that took them down to a walkway across grass lawns with borders of roses past their best. Areas of jungle were confined behind trellis-stone walls. In the middle of one of the borders a robot, the shape of a cone standing on its point with arms and appendages around its top edge, was pruning the roses. The path they walked on was rough-cut marble.

'This is a beautiful home you have here,' Karl observed.

'The best,' said Jarrol. 'It used to be a research base. We had it converted about a year back.... Here ...' He gestured to an arched entrance into the structure to the side of which was a low balcony. 'This is where you'll be staying. It was here they used to keep a number of aquariums. I've retained a few. I think you'll like it.'

Jarrol led through the arch and opened a palm-locked door to his right. The room beyond was octagonal and luxuriously furnished, with sofas set in a floor pit, the latest in entertainment systems, and hover tables. But Karl was more interested in a triptych of three aquarium walls. He dropped his travel bag on one of the white vat-leather sofas and walked to stand at the focus of the three walls. Jarrol and Celia stood behind him.

'Local life forms?' he asked.

'Yes, the seas here are very rich,' said Jarrol. 'Did you see the reefs on your way in?'

'I wondered.' Karl pointed at a creature like an armoured mouse that was creeping along the bottom of the tank. 'What about that?'

'Believe it or not it's called a mouse crab. Very much like Earth crustaceans in some ways, though there are three sexes and two very different kinds of DNA, one kind parasitic on the other.'

'At least they have DNA.'

As they watched, a creature like a miniature manta ray settled on the mouse crab. There was a struggle and the water went cloudy for a moment. As it cleared the little ray was gone. Pieces of carapace drifted through the water to be picked at by a shoal of mobile silver buttons.

'I guess you have to restock fairly regularly,' said Karl.

'No we don't,' said Jarrol.

Karl turned round to look at him then at Celia.

Celia explained, 'The tanks are connected into the system just like the swimming pool.'

Karl turned back to the tank.

'Then all these are blue hole dwellers?'

'Yes.'

'Then what the Hell is the sea like?' He turned back.

'I told you the seas were rich,' said Jarrol with a grin. 'Anyway, we'll leave you to settle in for a while, when you're ready we'll be by the pool.'

Jarrol headed for the door with Celia trailing behind.

'See you shortly,' said Karl.

Celia hung back as Jarrol left. At the door she brushed her damp hair back with her hands. She was sun-tanned and as near to naked as made no difference, her brown skin had a sheen of sweat, and the look she gave Karl could not have been mistaken for anything other than an invitation. As much as he hated to admit it, he was sorely tempted. She left with a flash of white teeth.

'AI,' said Karl when she had gone. 'Close the door.'

The door slid shut.

The pool was constructed to appear natural. The diving area was below what looked like a natural rock formation with a waterfall pouring down one side of it. As Karl walked out, to where Celia and Jarrol were sprawled on loungers, he saw someone on the topmost rock in silhouette against the darkening sky, and watched him dive. Augmented, Karl knew straight away.

'Impressive,' he said as he sprawled on the grass beside the couple.

'What ... David?' said Jarrol.

'No, the pool.'

'Oh,' Jarrol seemed momentarily at a loss. 'Would you like a drink?' he ventured.

'Please. Eldron Poteen if I may.'

Jarrol made no move but shortly a small AG tray floated out of the house with the drink on it. Karl took the drink and the tray hung about as if waiting for a tip before sliding away.

'I remember when all you used to drink was fruit juice,' said Celia.

'I've changed. It has been four years.'

'We all have ... I'm going for a swim.'

Karl watched her go, aware that she probably wanted him to join her in the pool, or was she playing her games with this David? Karl had still to figure who and what he was.

'When do you sleep here? I want to get in sync,' he asked.

'Some time soon. We've all been up for about twenty solstan hours.' Jarrol looked at him. 'It is good to see you Karl, and Secondnight we celebrate.'

'Secondnight?'

'Second half of the night. After we've slept. You'll get used to it.... Anyway, I've invited a lot of friends. It should be quite a party.'

'Anyone I know?'

'I'm not sure. A number of them are marine biologists.'

'No, I mean ... I was hoping Hilster, Burnet or Janer might be about. They know how to celebrate.'

There was a long silence.

'Janer left about four solstan months ago. I don't know where she is. Hilster and Burnet are dead.'

Karl downed all his drink and held up his empty glass. The tray came out with another drink for him. He gave it his empty glass and took the full one. The tray regarded him with its crystal eyes before sliding off again.

'Dead? How?'

'I though you knew. It happened about five months ago. We'd been diving for a few months when I realised it was going to take couple of decades to explore the blue holes here. That's when I bought this place. One day we went down and Hilster and Burnet just didn't come up again. We searched for ages and even sent remotes into the system. Couldn't find them.'

'You were using that antique scuba?'

'Yes, part of the challenge, you know that. With gills and monofilaments and the rest of that tech it gets too easy. We wanted a challenge.'

'What do you reckon happened?'

'Well, they were unroped. They must have gone into a silt- filled cavern and stirred things up. You know what happens. The water clouds, you panic, next thing you know you can't find where you came in.'

'Hilster and Burnet ... and you say no bodies?'

'No.'

'Surprising really. They were very professional when they were diving.'

'And very drunk when they were not,' said Jarrol.

Karl chuckled, then glanced toward the main residence as the exterior lights came on.
'I think Burnet was the noisiest but Hilster the craziest. You remember that bracelet he bought from that dealer on Ganymede? What was his name?'

'Don't remember.'

'Come on, you must do, you were the one who had the most dealings with him.'

'Oh yes, Jason Chel,' said Jarrol with a definite reluctance.

'Yes, he claimed he'd used it on himself didn't he?'

'Used what?' Celia had returned from the pool. She stood near to Karl as she dried herself with a large towel.

'Hilster's Four Season Changer, that bracelet. It was supposed to be a twenty-seventh century adaptogen laboratory,' said Karl.

'Chel,' she said. Karl nodded. Jarrol seemed intent on his drink. 'He did use it, and then he went through reconversion. You lot didn't find out about him. You were too interested in that scuba gear he was selling.'

Karl glanced at Jarrol, who now seemed to have no interest in the conversation, then looked back to Celia as she sat down on the grass next to him and continued to scrub the towel across her breasts.

'What happened?' he asked.

'He was on Scylla when the world-tide came. It was a case of adapt or die. He changed himself into an amalgam of man and murder-louse.'

Abruptly Jarrol said, 'This is all very interesting, but is not a subject I relish.'

'Sorry,' said Karl. 'It must have been a nightmare.'

'It was certainly that,' said Jarrol, staring into the falling night. Karl stood up and drained the last of his second drink.

'I think I'll get some sleep now. It was a tiring journey.'

'Every microsecond of it?' asked Celia.

Karl shook his head.

'The longest journeys are on either side of the runcible. In all I've been travelling for nine hours even though fifty-seven light years of the distance was covered in a microsecond. I'll wish you good night.'

'Good Firstnight to you, Karl,' said Jarrol.

'Dream sweetly,' said Celia.

It was strange, to get up after sleeping long and deeply, and walk out into electric lit midnight. No matter that he had slept for ten solstan hours, he still could not wake up properly. He felt dull, his head full of grey fog. He turned from the balcony and walked back into the apartment.

'AI, do you have any lag pills or biotrip?'

A mildly sensual voice replied.

'There is available a course of biorhythm changers to bring people in line with the days and nights of Arrived. Your hosts do not use them and I would advise you against using them. I suggest a stimulant.'

'Why the advice against?'

'The changers are a mild adaptogenic drug. They would cause you to sleep through the twenty hour night and be awake during the thirty hour day in this season. I was informed you are only here for a short stay. The changes in brain chemistry can be ... disconcerting.'

Karl laughed.

'Okay, I'll find another way to wake up. Give me a towel.'

I cupboard popped open to expose a stack of towels. Karl took one then went to his personal cupboard to get his shield goggles and swimming trunks. Suitably clad he headed for the pool. He knew he had an hour or so before anyone turned up.

The water was warm and slightly salt. As he surfaced it was shed by the repellent energy band across his eyes. He slid into an easy crawl and covered the fifty-metre length of the pool in a minute and started back. Twenty lengths later he spotted David sitting on the edge of the pool watching him. He swam over to him and stood up in the shallows.

'You swim very well.'

'I like to stay in trim.'

'Jarrol says you're unaugmented.'

'Never felt the need.'

David ran his eyes over Karl's body then stood up. He was naked. 'I think I'll join you.'

Karl had nothing against nakedness, but he was profoundly hetero and did not like the way David was watching him.

'Well, I'm done now. I'd best get ready for when the guests arrive. See you in a bit.'

He climbed out of the pool and headed back to his apartment, feeling David's eyes on him all the way. As he came to the arch he sensed another person. He looked to the balcony. Celia.

'You've been at the pool with our lovely David then?'

Karl climbed the steps to the balcony and looked at her. She sat on one of the loungers and had a drink in her hand. Now she wore a dress that clung to her every curve and ended mid-thigh. Her hair was up and she had a light touch of make-up on her face.

'Who is he?' he asked.

'A friend of Jarrol's. They get along very well together.'

There was bitterness in her voice.

'Why is he here?'

Celia replied with irony. 'For the party of course.'

Karl entered his apartment, stripped off his trunks and goggles and took a shower. As he sluiced off the salt water he knew he would probably make no objection if she joined him. She did not. After showering he dressed in a monofilament overall, got himself a cup of coffee, and walked back out onto the balcony.

'You dislike me, don't you Karl.'

Karl laughed. 'Too strong. You make me uncomfortable.'

'I'm sorry.'

He looked at her. 'Well back-off a bit then.'

Celia stared down into her drink for a moment then gazed up at him with a pained expression.

'You don't know what it's been like here.'

'It's not only here. Remember the Titanic II?'

She bowed her head. 'It's different now.' She stood. 'I wish we could be friends. I don't have any here.' She walked out into the night.

Still trying to make some sense out of the conversation Karl drank a second coffee and was part way through the third when he heard the first of the AGCs arrive. He walked outside and joined Jarrol and Celia on the roofport. The first guests to arrive were a family of four: a husband and wife with two teenage daughters. The parents were both marine biologists and Karl soon found himself sitting on the grass at the edge of the pool with them, deep in discussion about the local marine life. The daughters headed directly to the waterfall, which it turned out was a disguised water-slide. Overhead, AGCs arrived one after the other. A group of youths in a Porsche replica buzzed low over the pool yelling halloos. Karl observed one of the teenage girls throwing them a finger. Soon the grounds were scattered with noisy groups of people, music was playing from the house, holodancers were pirouetting across the lawns. The air swarmed with floating drink trays.

'The pool's getting crowded,' Karl observed.

Jennifer Singhe, the wife of the husband and wife team, shook her head and took a sip of her drink. 'Yes, so it would appear. How strange that most of them are young men.'

'Best keep an eye on your daughters then,' said Karl.

Morris Singhe let out a bark of laughter. His wife glanced at him and smiled. She looked at Karl and observed his surprise.

'I see,' she said, understanding. 'We thought you were one of Jarrol's young men. Our daughters are quite safe I assure you. Though I think they would prefer not to be.'

Karl closed his hand into a fist and thumped it against his forehead. Celia's bitterness. David...

'I've been unforgivably thick,' he said.

Jennifer pointed. 'Here comes the grand Oscar now.'

Jarrol walked to the edge of the pool in his baggy shorts. A number of youths were yelling at him from the water. He struck a pose at the edge then climbed the steps up to the diving rocks. Karl watched him arrow down into the water just as the Singhe daughters ran up.

'Dad! Mother! There's something in there! Something at the bottom!'

Karl flicked his attention back to the pool as suddenly people were getting out very quickly. Somebody was screaming. He stood so he could see what was going on. There was a panic. More screaming.

'Where's Jarrol?'

Morris Singhe stood at his side. 'Can't see him. I saw him go in...'

'What could be down there? What could have gotten in from the caves?'

'Nothing big. There's a grating across.'

Karl turned to the girls. 'What did you see? What did it look like?'

'Like ... like a man ... sort of ...'

Some kind of practical joke gone wrong? This seemed the type of crowd. Jarrol still had not come up. Karl ran for the pool, hit the water in a flat dive, and swam at full speed to the diving area. There he submerged. Vision blurred. If only he had brought his shield goggles out. He swam down through the floodlit water. Pressure crushed his sinuses, made his ears ache. There: the grating. Two shapes, both men. He swam down to them and saw that one of the figures being dragged to the grating by the other. He recognised the one being dragged as Jarrol. The other one had some kind of suit on. He swam into them, grabbed Jarrol round the waist and planted his foot against the other. Luminescent white eyes glared at him. He shoved, but nothing seemed to happen. A grey eel-flesh arm pushed against his chest and a webbed and clawed hand came up before his eyes. The head that jutted above him was not human. It was shaped like a lizard's. Spined fins jutted from the body. The clawed hand closed around his throat and the head moved closer. A mouth filled with back-slanted shark's teeth opened. Then suddenly he was released, still holding Jarrol. As he headed for the surface he saw the creature dart down through the grating. The plasticrete bars had been broken.

'How is he?'
    Celia slumped into the white sofa and took the drink Karl proffered. 'The AI's monitoring him. Minimal brain damage, but its keeping him in the cold-coffin until it's run a complete check. David's with him.'
    'I talked with Morris and Jennifer Singhe. They tell me they don't think there's anything in the oceans like the creature I saw, but apparently there are blue holes on every land mass. Arrived is a regular Swiss cheese. No one has fully catalogued the life forms in the underwater caves.'
    Celia stared into her drink.

'I wonder if that's what got Hilster and Burnet? I always thought it strange the two of them disappearing like that,' she said, something in the tone of her voice Karl could not figure.

'It seemed quite capable. It smashed through a plasticrete grating.' Karl sat down on the sofa opposite her. 'Why do you stay, Celia?'

She gazed up and stared at him with disconcerting intensity. 'So you've finally figured it out. You're very slow sometimes, Karl.'

'The academic life. It makes you naive. You still haven't answered my question.'

Celia drained her drink then filled it from the bottle on the side table. 'Scotch whisky. The academic life must pay well.' She looked at him carefully. 'It's my house. I like it here.'

'You own the house? But ... why do you stay with Jarrol?'

Celia peered at him then looked away. She did not answer. None of his business. Karl sipped his drink and thought about it for a moment.

'This has been an experience for me. Having my illusions destroyed one after the other. One should never try to relive the past,' he said.

He lay back on the sofa and stared across the room at the aquarium. Celia stood, walked to stand over him. Abruptly she put her drink down on the table and sat astride his hips.

'How about we live the now?' she said, and hauled her dress up and over her head.

All his previous objections were irrelevant, Karl decided. He slid his hands up her thighs, her flat stomach, caressed her breasts for a moment, then slid his fingers into her hair. He pulled her down.

Karl struggled to the surface of deep black sleep. Something was striving to gain his attention. He heard a rattling clicking, water dulled and shrouded by the white-noise bubbling of the aquarium. He woke to the damp warmth of a body pressed against his own and thought perhaps she had woken him. But the sound continued, clicking, scraping. He opened his eyes and slid himself upright, trying not to rouse Celia. Nothing, nothing in the room. Then he saw the white eyes staring out at him from the aquarium, heard the sound of claws rattling and scraping across the thick glass.

Very quietly he said, 'AI, can you close the vents to the aquarium?'

'This is not possible,' the AI replied in its usual voice.

'What? What?' said Celia.

Karl pointed out their visitor to her.

'Oh Christ! Make it go away!'

Karl glanced at her, surprised at her reaction. There was at least an inch of safety glass between them and the creature and it probably could not survive out of water anyway.

'AI, do the vents to this aquarium open out directly into the cave system?'

'One of them does. The other opens to the swimming pool which it uses as a cistern.'

'Very well. Turn the lights on please.'

The lights came on and Karl got a good look at the creature before it swam to the side of the tank and was gone. He leapt out of the sofa.

'Jesus!'

He dragged on some trousers and headed for the door.

'What's wrong? What's going on?'

Karl ignored her. He went out through the door and ran for the pool. The lights were dimmer outside now as the slow dawn appeared. The blimp moon rose for the third and last time that night. Karl slowed as he reached the grass, diverted to something that rested on the edge of the pool – a damp anomalous bundle. Had the creature climbed out? As he came near to it the stink made him gag and abruptly he realised what he was looking at: an antique scuba diving suit containing a badly decayed corpse, one flipper missing, mask broken, tangled in nylon rope, white flatworms squirming in the empty eye-sockets. It was six months old, Karl knew. Its decay had probably been slowed by the lack of the right kind of bacteria here. He squatted down next to it, pulled on the nylon rope, and inspected the severed end. After a moment he stood up and stared into the pool. The creature was there, watching him. He turned away and headed back.

'Celia,' he said as he stepped into his apartment. 'I need—'

A hand struck him across the side of his face and he hit the floor coming near to black-out.

'You treacherous bastard!'

Karl looked up into the face that sneered down at him. Jarrol. He glanced across and saw Celia sitting on the sofa. David had her hair gripped in one hand. She looked terrified.

'What was that for?' Karl asked calmly. He realised this was a situation that needed calm. Jarrol was just as augmented as David. If it came to it, they would be able to tear him apart, literally. A foot struck him in the stomach, but he had been expecting it and it was not as bad as it could have been.

'I let you come here as a friend and you screw my wife!'

Karl felt his anger growing. This was the man whose life he had saved earlier. The man who now had no sexual interest in his wife.

'Well perhaps she was tired of taking it up the ass.'

Jarrol's face went ugly with rage. Karl rolled aside as Jarrol's foot stamped down where his face would have been. He tried to get up but was not quick enough. He only caught some of the force of the blow on his chest, but it lifted him from his feet and dropped him back on a floating table. The field crackled under the table and it slid out of position. He gasped for breath. Jarrol stamped down again and Karl rolled aside again. The table shattered and fell to the floor.

'Burnet...' Karl managed, and lay gasping waiting for the next blow. After a moment he peered up at Jarrol and met his insane glare.

'What about Burnet?' Jarrol asked, slowly, viciously.

Karl pushed himself to his knees and felt his ribs. None of them seemed broken.

'He's out there, by the pool.'

Jarrol suddenly looked frightened. 'What do you mean?'

'What I say.' Karl climbed to his feet and stood swaying. 'Burnet is out there lying by the pool. His corpse.'

Jarrol stared at him then abruptly stepped forward and hit him. Blackness descended like a falling wall.

He woke with his head a ball of pain and the taste of vomit in his mouth. As soon as he lifted his head and tried to open his eyes he retched and blackness threatened again. Eventually he managed to get his eyes open while keeping vomit down. He was tied in one of the loungers dragged in from the balcony. Celia was sitting on the sofa. He surveyed the room. Jarrol and David were gone. He focused on Celia and she looked up.

'Untie me.'

Celia appeared frightened, guilty. She had been crying and her face was bruised. Blood was crusted round her mouth.

'It killed them. It killed Hilster and Burnet,' she said.

'Is that what Jarrol told you?'

She stared at the floor and wrung her hands together. Karl gritted his teeth against another surge of sickness. The room steadied.

'It's a lie, Celia. Jarrol told me they went down unroped. The corpse out there had a safety rope attached to it, and the end had been cut, probably with a chainglass knife.'

Celia's face creased up. She was crying again, quietly. Karl stared at her estimatingly.

'But you knew that didn't you? Or you suspected. Why did he do it? Did one of them react badly to his advances? Reject him? Come on, tell me Celia. What was it they did?' He paused to gauge the effect of his words, then went on.

'I suppose Jarrol was telling the truth to a certain extent. I bet they did go into a silted-up cave, but they went roped. He cut their ropes. What sin was so bad they must be punished by slow suffocation then drowning? Do you reckon they felt they deserved their fate as they watched the air dials drop to zero, as they took their first breaths of muddy water?'

'I can't,' Celia wailed, and began bawling.

Karl peered up at the ceiling. 'AI, are you there?'

There was no response. Jarrol had disabled it. Karl returned his attention to Celia.

'You can't ... I don't suppose it matters. After disposing of Burnet's remains Jarrol will be back for me. He'll figure I've worked it out when he sees the rope. My corpse will probably end up in a cavern, another death to attribute to ... your creature.'

Karl glanced bitterly towards the aquarium.

'It was Hilster,' Celia managed through her sobs. 'We had an affair ... I was going to leave with him.'

'Christ.' He stared back at her. 'Earlier on you accused me of being slow on the uptake. You're slower still. Jarrol is hanging onto you because of your money, plain and simple. There can be no other explanation. How long before you meet with an accident? How long before your body disappears somewhere? It's got to stop. For Chrissake untie me! It won't take them long to lose Burnet!'

'They're ... That's not what they're doing.'

Karl waited. 'They've gone after the creature.'

Karl closed his eyes. Time to play the ace he had been holding back.

'Shit, Celia, if you loved Hilster, untie me.'

She shook her head. Looked confused.

'For Chrissake wake up!' He glared at her. 'Why do you think Burnet's body suddenly appeared? Who put it there? Jesus! That's not some previously undetected life form they've gone after, it's Hilster! He used the bracelet! He used the Four Seasons Changer!'

Celia stared at him in shock. 'Hilster?'

'Jarrol has gone to tie up a loose end, and no doubt when he has done that he'll come back here and tie up a few more, so to speak.'

Karl looked pointedly at his bonds. Celia stood up. 'That can't be Hilster.'

'Don't be thick, Celia. You're the one that found out about Jason Chel. You know it's possible. Anyway, I saw the bracelet on his wrist when he was in the aquarium. It's Hilster.'

Celia rubbed her hands on the front of her dress. 'What ... what can we do?'

'You untie me and I'll go after them. I might not be augmented, but I'm probably better in the water than that David. Perhaps I can divert them away ... something. First we call in the local enforcers, police, whatever, and if possible call in a Monitor. There must be at least one in the city.'

'Hilster was augmented.'

Karl thought about the broken grating at the bottom of the pool. It figured. He gazed at Celia and waited. She stood over him for a moment, then abruptly ran out of the apartment. He swore and struggled to free himself. The knots had been pulled tight by augmented muscles though and he knew he did not stand a chance. The lounger went over on its side just as Celia returned. She squatted down before him with a chainglass knife glittering in her hand. Karl swallowed dryly. She seemed just as deranged as Jarrol. He breathed a sigh of relief when she cut his bonds, then stood up and groaned as the circulation returned to his arms and feet.

'Jarrol's disabled the AI, I take it?'

Celia nodded.

'Do you have a comcon?'

'Yes, but it is palm keyed to Jarrol.'

'Plans ahead doesn't he?' said Karl sarcastically. 'I suppose the AGCs are keyed as well. No doubt you cannot use them.'

Celia nodded again, shamefaced.

'Is there any way we can get in contact with the city, the police, anyone?'

Celia abruptly turned and ran from the room. Karl followed her out into light. The sun was rising. She ran to the pool, hesitated by the corpse, then ran to the diving rocks. They both climbed to the top where she pointed out to sea.

'Morris and Jennifer.'

Moored out beyond the reef was a large research vessel.

'Studying the reef,' said Karl. 'How long have they been out there?'

'Four months.'

'They're probably what kept you alive. Get them. Set fire to the fucking house if you have to, but get them.'

'I think we have flares.'

But Karl was already on the way down.

Back in his apartment Karl pulled a monofilament body suit from his cupboard, his shield goggles, a set of flippers, a torch and a gill. Quickly he pulled on the suit and fixed the gill round his neck with the mouthpiece dangling down his chest, then he put on the goggles and rooted through his belongings again. A long chrome bar came to light. A shock stick. It could deter a Great White but what about an augmented human? It was all he had. He slung his flippers over his shoulder and headed for the pool. Celia was nowhere about, but as he pulled on the flippers and stuck the breather in his mouth an actinic red star shot into the sky. Vessel in distress. Karl dived in.

It was murky at the bottom of the pool and a yellow plastic-clad monofilament led from the edge of the grating into the cave system. Karl followed it into the darkness and flicked on his torch. The beam picked out nacreous crustaceans clinging to the rocks, blue sea-lettuces, shoals of button-fish. The filament led him into a long tunnel that spiralled down then back up again. His ears were ringing and he wished he had remembered his ear-plugs. Too late now. The tunnel remained level for a while then went down again. There were chambers on either side. The beam revealed a ray like a spread cloak hanging in one of them. He swam on quickly.

Further along and he found a chainglass harpoon buried in the rock wall. The tunnel branched and he stayed with the filament.

More branches and more twists. Chambers above, below, either side, other tunnels curving off into darkness. Karl checked his watch and saw he had been down for half an hour. His entire body ached and he was not so sure Jarrol had not broken a rib. He swam on for another half hour then stopped to check the gill display on his shoulder. The readings were good. He had two more hours before the activated haemoglobin started to break down. Two and a half if he pushed it. He swam on for ten minutes more until he saw a tangle of yellow before him in the murk. Quickly he pulled himself behind a rock and watched. No movement. He approached cautiously. Jarrol.

Some of the cladding had been stripped from the filament and it had cut into his chest like a cheese wire. His gill had been ripped away and he hung in the water with his mouth wide open and his eyes bulging. Karl realised that the murk surrounding him was blood. He observed movement in Jarrol's suit and pulled it open. Mouse-crabs fed. He swam on, growing more uneasy the further he got from the filament. Was he safe from Hilster? How much of Hilster had survived adaptation? How much of his brain was left? Suddenly he saw David swim across before him, fast, terrified. He kicked after him and tried to catch him. Tunnel, chamber, another tunnel. It was no good. David was soon out of sight, his augmented muscles propelling him along like a torpedo. At least it seemed as if Hilster was safe. Karl turned and swam back. Tunnel, chamber, tunnel, back into the original tunnel and back to Jarrol and the filament. Only Jarrol was not there and Karl suddenly did not know where he was.

He tried not to panic. Panic used up oxygen. He retraced his path and found that yet again he did not recognise where he was. That bunch of weed, was it the same one he had seen earlier, but from the other side? Perhaps he had turned around? Was it further than this? Had he chased after David for longer than he had thought? He paused at a cage of weed covered stalactites and tried to control his breathing. He swam back and tried to think logically, but soon realised he was completely lost. Blue holes. There were loads of blue holes scattered across the peninsula. If he kept swimming and kept taking the paths upward he was sure to find one. He peered at his watch. Hour and a half to go, pushing it.

The gill surface turned from red to purple on its way to blue. Four times he had taken a tunnel only to have it curve down. Three times he had run into dead ends. He did not need to check his watch to know he was running out of time. It was becoming increasingly difficult to breath, he was cold, and so very tired. At the fourth dead-end he found David, bug-eyed, mouth gaping, fingers driven into the blue surfaces of his gill. He and Jarrol had gone in about half an hour ahead of Karl. This is what awaited him in that time. He swam out, gasping raggedly as he drew oxygen from the failing gill. White flashes passed before his eyes ... only they were not white flashes. They were white eyes. Something knocked the shock-stick from his hand.

Karl tried to fight against a body that was cybernetically augmented and adapted to underwater life. It was a pointless exercise that used up valuable oxygen. A hand like an iron clamp closed about his arm and he was dragged along faster than even David had been able to swim. The torch tumbled away into the depths. Where was it taking him? He saw a flash of yellow and knew hope. The line. He had to remember this was Hilster, this creature was Hilster. He blacked out for a moment then and came to, struggling to pull out his mouthpiece. The iron hand secured both his wrists and pulled him along. A remote drone buzzed past, stayed with them.

At last, the grating, for a moment. Blackness. Light. Figures swimming in the water, taking hold of him, pulling him up. He blacked out again, then was gasping good clean air, his skin warmed by bright sunlight.

The ECM was a woman from a Heavy G world. She seemed young and innocuous in the plain grey Monitor's uniform, but Karl was well aware that the agents of Earth Central were the toughest and most capable human beings around, when they were human. She gave him a cup of hot coffee laced with brandy and waited patiently for him to get his wits about him. He pulled the blanket closer around his shoulders and glanced at the Arrived police scattered around the grounds, at the tarpaulin covered shape at the end of the pool. Then he looked into the pool where Hilster could be seen lurking.

'You okay?' she asked him eventually.

He nodded. She turned on a recorder on her belt.

'The full story please.'

He told her, missing out nothing, even his brief liaison with Celia.

'It was an opportunist's murder then, else Burnet would not have had to die,' she said.

'He would have known about the ropes. Jarrol could not let him live. He might have had some idea what was going on between Celia and Hilster, and Jarrol's reaction.'

'It would seem this Jarrol did not need so much justification for murder. He was probably psychotic.'

Karl nodded.

'Where is Celia now?'

'She was taken back to the city for psychiatric evaluation.'

Karl nodded. Again: it figured.

The Monitor looked into the pool. 'You realise how lucky you were?'

'Yes.'

She glanced at him. 'There could well have been nothing of the man you knew left. Adaptation takes some time and he was almost certainly drowning when it happened. He was probably brain damaged.'

'What will happen to him?'

'It is unlikely he'll be charged with anything.' She turned when one of the officers came running over.

'She's there,' said the man.

'Who?' asked Karl glancing from one to the other.

The Monitor's expression had turned steely. 'Another part of this jigsaw, though I dislike to draw an analogy with something so tidy. We reconnected the AI and discovered another of this Jarrol's little secrets. Come.'

Karl stood and on unsteady legs followed her across the lawns. She led him to an area where a number of officers stood round a hole excavated by a small mechanical digger. He looked down into the hole and saw human remains.

'Janer MacAllen. Perhaps you have some idea why he killed her,' said the Monitor.

'I was told she went off-planet,' said Karl. 'Like Burnet she probably had some idea of what Jarrol was planning. She probably heard something or saw something. Perhaps she voiced doubts about Hilster and Burnet's accident. She would have known neither of them would enter a cavern unroped.'

'Just so: paranoid psychotic.'

Karl turned away, shaking his head. He felt so very tired. He walked back to the pool and gazed down at Hilster while trying to remember the good times. They would not come clear in his mind. Shortly the Monitor rejoined him, a notescreen in her hand, which she held out to him. Printed across it were the words, 'We can reverse the adaptation.'

'Water-proof,' she said, and tossed the screen into the pool.

A few minutes passed, then the screen was lifted out of the water by a webbed and clawed hand. The words, 'About bloody time.' were printed on it. Karl laughed, surprised that he was able to.

ENDS

DRAGON IN THE FLOWER

A scream, silent in underspace – a flicker of existence between the shadows of stars. It is known, the scream, but quince never remember. For Cormac there was merely a flash of black and red, a Dante glimpse, and he was completing his thought far from where he began it.

 -on mince and slices of quince which they ate with a runcible spoon. Is that right?

 Times change: terms change, and it was an ancient nonsense rhyme. He was well aware of that as he fought to overcome the disorientation of mitter-lag.

 And the runcible spoon flicks them across the galaxy ... Hah! Myths rewritten. I'm a knight in shining armour only my hardware's on the inside.

 Caught in the flaw of a jewel Cormac considered dragons. Ten seconds and four hundred light years later his mind caught up with his body. The scream was lost in a twilight place. Echoes. He stepped from the shimmer of the cusp. Down the steps from the pedestal, across the black-glass floor, then out of the containment sphere.

 'Ian Cormac?'

 'Yes.'

 The sky was metallic red, the land pink rock with black striations. The curve to horizon was different. He sneezed then breathed deeply. The air tasted salt, and silica dust coated his tongue. After a moment of deliberation he turned his attention to the speaker.

 'I am Maria,' said the girl who's hair was red with no white light to show him different. Cormac held out his hand to silence her as his breath gouted in the chill air like lung-blood. He continued to look around.

Wasteland. Beautiful as rubies, scabrous as rust, dead as them both.

He gestured back at the runcible.

'Only one. Quince and light cargo. Few people come here,' he observed.

'Yes, Dragon set a limit of twenty thousand visitors a year.'

'Solstan year?'

'No ... Colora,' she said, annoyed.

Cormac stared at her.

'I require assistance, not impatience,' he said, and waited.

'Yes, Ambassador' she said grudgingly, rubbing her hand on a leather-sheathed hip. Cormac accessed his link:

<u>Maria Convala.</u> *Born on Aster Colora 2376 solstan, exobiologist attached to the Earth Central study team, ambitious, has connections with the Separatist movement, is rumoured to have been involved in the third Jovian putsch...*

He smiled bleakly and turned his attention to the iron slug of an AGC that had been left on hover nearby. He noted the rust streaks, and the plates welded to its underside.

Old.

Such was always the way this far from Earth. Things broke down, wore out, were infrequently replaced. He should consider himself lucky they had AGCs here at all.

'Shall we go?' he said, after a pause.

As they slid above the desolation Cormac accessed information more relevant to his task. There was no life here but for the human colony, the sentient Dragon, and the insentient Monitor (the latter two leviathans) nor had there been. There were no fossils, chalk deposits, or life-based hydrocarbons, nothing. That raised the as yet unanswered questions; where was the ecology

Dragon and Monitor had evolved from? Was it on Aster Colora?

Dragon had immediately communicated with those first to arrive through the seed-ship runcible, and had been in continuous communication with the colony ever since, yet, little had been learnt about it.

'Has Dragon given reasons for its request?'

'It was more of a demand than a request.'

'Clarify that.'

With her hand resting on the guide-ball of the AGC Maria glanced at him.

'We have always been here on sufferance. It said, 'Send me an Ambassador' there was no request.'

Cormac noted the bitterness. As a Separatist, he realised, this put her in an intolerable position. How could she campaign for political independence while Aster Colora could not rise above colony status?

The redland flowed under the rock of the AGC until at length Cartis, like a spreading fungus, came into view. Like any tourist Cormac booked into the Metrotel. In his room he slumped on his bed and accessed Dragon/Human dialogue. Human politics was irrelevant in this case, which for Cormac, was a novelty.

'You continue to evade our questions concerning yourself,' said a man only just holding onto his temper.

'Yes, this is true,' came the indifferent reply.

'Yet for years you have had access to our information systems. You know our history, the level of our technology ... You perhaps know more about the human race than any single member of it. Why will you not tell us about yourself? Surely, this is little to ask?'

'You are correct: I know more about you people than any

single member of your kind.'

'You have not answered my question.'

'Yes I have.'

'I do not understand.'

'A very human trait.'

'Please explain.'

'The runcible has been developed to the stage where it is near perfect in function. Humankind can now step from star system to star system with ease. On Earth, contra terrene power is about to be introduced. In the system of Cassius the first Dyson sphere is under construction. The matter for this project came from a planet of Jovian size, demolished by a contra terrene missile.'

'Do you fear us.'

'Should I?'

'Many assume that this is the reason for your reticence.'

'How old are you, Darson?'

'One hundred and seventy, solstan.'

'It is likely that you will live to be over eight hundred years old and then only to die of ennui.'

'Perhaps. How old are you?'

'Do you represent your race, Darson?'

'In the sense-'

'No, you do not represent your race. I cannot sit in judgment on you. Send me an Ambassador.'

After the dialogue had ceased, Cormac opened his eyes and scratched at his head. He was tired, he had, after all, travelled a long way. He got off the bed and shed the clothes he had been wearing only a few hours earlier, personal time, in New York, and wondered, as always with cold humour, what the morning might bring. Of course he did not know whether it was day or night here, but such things he had dismissed as irrelevant over the last five years. He lived by personal time. It was the only way to stay sane.

The morning brought Maria with an analysis from Darson, the Dragon expert. Cormac read it over a breakfast of spiced eggs, honeyfish, and two pots of tea. Darson's conclusion was that Dragon, in human terms, was insane. After reading it Cormac dressed in his shabby survival suit and placed in his rucksack the single device he might need. On his way out he consigned the report to the waste disposal. Shortly he was sliding above redland, red, under a bloody sky.

'What is your opinion of Darson?'

'He's a pompous old fart,' Maria replied, and Cormac liked her for that.

'He believes Dragon is psychotic.'

'I am not qualified to judge.'

Expressionlessly Cormac watched pink snow melt and slide off the frictionless screen of the AGC.

'You are qualified to have an opinion.'

Maria hesitated before replying. Cormac glanced at her and could see her discomfort. She was, he knew, trying to decide how to try and influence him and what opinion it would be best to own. He repressed a smile. She was in a difficult position. Instructions had preceded him: no unnecessary contact, straight to Dragon, the crux. He could see that she was unnerved.

'The dialogue with Dragon is deceptively human ... Darson seems to find it difficult to accept the alien.'

Cormac chuckled. The AGC dipped as Maria glanced at him quickly. Unable to find any way of applying leverage she had answered with the truth. He nodded to himself and looked ahead as she slowed the AGC and began to power it down.

Before them lay The Junkyard. This was the tangible result of people flouting Dragon's rule of no machinery larger than a man within a two kilometre radius of it. Many people had died here. Maria put the AGC on hover. Cormac tapped the com on his belt as the door slid open.

'I'll contact you when I want picking up,' he said and left her.

After reaching the line of smashed AGCs and hover scooters that marked the two kilometre boundary Cormac shouldered his rucksack and climbed a rusting hulk. Even through the snow the four spheres were visible, standing like vast storage tanks on a plain of broken rock. After a moment he clambered down the other side of the boundary, peeking in the wrecked AGC at the occupants no one had bothered to retrieve. As his feet touched the ground, the ground moved.

Pseudopods.

He stood very still and waited, the taste of salt turning acrid in his mouth. Five metres to one side of him the ground rippled and a thing like a metre-wide cobra exploded into the air. Cormac dropped to avoid flying rock, rolled, looked up. It arched above him, a single crystalline blue eye where a cobra's mouth should have been. The ground tilted and another explosion followed. Then another. Cormac put his rucksack over his head as explosion followed explosion and he was pelted with shards of rock. Then it ceased, and he stood, in silence.

Hydra would have been better.

Arrayed and curved like the ribs of an immense snake's skeleton the pseudopods had become his honour guard. He walked down the spine.

In the face of total disaster defiance is the only recourse ... crazy street-lamps they have here.

Cormac allowed his mind to wander – random access on

subject:

Monitor: <u>Monitor:</u> *Insentient autochthon of the planet Aster Colora. It has the appearance of a Terran monitor lizard but is a kilometre long and weighs an estimated four point five million tonnes. It is a silicon based life form with an alien physiognomy...*

Dragon ... Monitor ... What connection?
Why does Dragon want an Ambassador?
Questions.
Answers?
Damn!

The two kilometres unrolled and eventually Cormac came before the curving edifice of tegulate flesh in an amphitheatre of pseudopods. He noted, to one side, a piece of machinery that could have been the comlink for Dragon/Human dialogue. The one exception to its rule about machines. It was scrapped. He looked up at the pink and red-stippled sky, half cut by cloud-tangled flesh mountain, and he waited.

'Ambassador.'

The voice came from the undershadows of the sphere, resonant but conversational.

'Ian Cormac ... yes.'

'Names. All things can be named.'

As of skis on granular snow, a hissing issued from the undershadows. Cormac saw a swirl of movement then a monstrous head shot towards him propelled by a ribbed snake body. He stumbled back, fell. It rose above him: a pterosaur head with sapphire eyes.

'Are you afraid?'

Cormac choked back his immediate reply and said, 'Should I be?' His tone betrayed nothing of what he felt.

The head lunged at him then jerked to a halt two metres

above him. It smelt of cloves. Milky saliva dripped on him.

'Answer my question.'

'Yes, I am afraid. Does that surprise you?'

'No.'

The head moved up and away. Cormac stood and brushed himself off.

'I fail to see the purpose of that little scene,' he said.

'You represent your race,' Dragon replied, 'and you can die.'

More than personal.

Cormac did not react to the implications but looked steadily into those sapphire eyes.

'Why did you send for an Ambassador.'

'Ah ... you *are* human then?'

'Of course.'

'You *do* represent your race?'

'Such is my position, though I cannot speak for every individual.' He emphasised 'individual'. Why? He did not know. It had almost been instinctive. The Dragon head swayed then switched, shaking off an accumulation of snow.

'Running round the inside of your skull is a net of mycorhizal fibre optics connected to etched-atom processors, silicon synaptic interfaces, and an underspace transmitter. Evolution is a wonderful thing,' it said.

How the Hell!

Quickly Cormac said, 'They are the tools of my trade. *I am human.* I am a member of the races of homo sapiens – wise man – and a wise man will use what tools he can to make his tasks easier.'

'I am glad you are sure of your integrity.'

The head swayed to one side then looked back. The tegulate flesh of the Dragon's body bulged and quivered as if it were taking a breath. There was a liquid groaning, then the tegulate skin parted like that of a rotten fruit. Unable to hide his reaction Cormac retched at the stench that wafted from the pink vagina of a cave that appeared before him. There were more liquid sounds driven by deep rhythmic pulses. Cormac watched in fascination as a jet of steaming amniot ejected the foetal ball of a manthing wrapped in a caul. The caul burst open, spilling more of the Dragon's juices. Dracoman. Cormac named it instantly.

'A trifle dramatic,' he managed.

The man continued to move. It stood, showing no sign of imbalance. Again that sound. Something else born: a flattened ellipse. The man picked it up and stripped away its caul. Legs dropped down from underneath it. Cormac could hardly believe he was looking at a table. The man approached and placed the table between them.

'To be human is to be mortal,' said Dragon. 'Do you play chess?'

'Yes I—'

Movement from the table: a bulging, bubbling, like sprouting mushrooms a Dragon chess set grew from its surface.

'Your move.'

For a moment Cormac could think of nothing else to say or do. He reached down and took hold of a pawn. The thing writhed in his hand, bit him. He yelled and dropped it. On the board it slithered forwards to a tegulate square.

'There is always a price for power,' said Dragon.

Cormac swore, then waited for his opponents move, his confusion growing.

Why? What purpose? A megalomaniacal game or a test?
He hoped for the latter.

As he thought he looked into his opponents eyes. The

dracoman betrayed nothing, even when he suddenly moved and brought his fist down on Cormac's pawn. Cormac was taken aback.

'That his not in the rule book,' he said, then damned himself for saying it. He knew what Dragon's reply would be.

'There are no rules here, just judgments.'

Probing...

Cormac decided to react. He brought his fist down and crushed his opponent's king.

'Check,' he said dryly, and watched his opponent.

The dracoman stared at the board for a moment then methodically began to crush every one of Cormac's pieces. White gore dribbled off the side of the table. Cormac turned towards the head.

'Surely by now you have enough insight into basic human reactions? You've been studying us for centuries,' he said.

'Every human is an individual, as you so rightly indicated,' observed Dragon.

Cormac was not sure that he had done any such thing. He turned back to his opponent.

'I do not like subjective games,' he said, and knocked the table aside. The dracoman went for him with frightening speed. The hands reaching for his throat he was able to knock aside, but he was knocked to the ground. The hands reached for his throat again. He brought his knee up then flung the clammy body from him. He regained his feet as his opponent did. The attack was still without finesse, and this time, not caught unawares, Cormac used his feet to counter it. The fight was over in seconds and the dracoman gurgling on the shale.

'Your second to last move was the wrong one.'

'I won.'

'That is not the issue.'

'What is?'

'Morality.'

'Hah, it is the winners who write history and it is the winners who invent morality. Existence is all the reason for existence any of us has, unless you believe in gods. I think you set yourself up too high.'

'No higher than an executioner.'

'You threaten again. Why? Do you have the power to carry out your threats? Do you think that you are a god?'

'I do not threaten you.'

'You seek to judge me then, to judge what I represent.'

'In the system of Betelgeuse there is a physicist working on some of the later Skaidon formulae. I predict he will solve some of the problems he has set himself.'

'And?'

'Within the next century the human race will have the intergalactic runcible.'

What!?

The ground shook. A vast shadow blotted out half the sky. With his skin crawling Cormac turned, and there, making its ponderous gargantuan way across the rockscape he saw the Monitor, long as a city, its legs like tower blocks. Cormac watched it pass, knew its destination.

'Another threat?' he breathed. 'What is it that you want?'

The head rose higher and gazed in the direction the Monitor had gone.

'Go back to Cartis. When you have seen what you must see, return here.'

Suddenly the head dropped down and was before Cormac.

'I control Monitor, without me it is mindless, but you know that,' it said, 'I have the power, the power to destroy. Could it be that you know what I mean?'

'I know the substance of your threat ... your warning?' was Cormac's reply. After a pause he looked down at the now unmoving Dracoman. Then he looked down at his rucksack, back up at Dragon, shrugged and walked away, random accessing as he did so, so nothing could be read from his expression:

Aster Colora: A planet on the rim of the galaxy.

Maria had been waiting for him at the two kilometre boundary. She was panicked, out of her depth.

'The whole city ... Monitor...'

Cormac silenced her and took her place in the driving seat of the AGC. Halfway back to Cartis she had calmed enough to be coherent.

'Pseudopods broke through all round the city. I was outside when it happened ... No one can escape and Monitor is heading in that direction. It has never done that before.'

'Dragon controls Monitor.'

'Why is it doing this?'

'Either it tests us or Darson is right.'

'Thanks for the comfort.'

Cartis was indeed ringed by pseudopods, but they parted to allow the AGC through. At the Metrotel Cormac used Maria's intentions and fear to get her to bed. He felt no remorse. She had been quite prepared to use him in any way she could for the Separatist movement. Lying on his bed he listened as the rumble of Monitor's arrival ceased, then he looked at the naked form lying beside him.

An affirmation of humanity?

The question was irrelevant. All waited on him.

Careful not to wake Maria, Cormac got off the bed and went to the bathroom. Ritualistically he shaved, cleaned his teeth, and dressed. He then sat down and accessed the runcible grid.

Earth Central.
Dragon intergalactic.
Proven?
To my satisfaction.

With that he sent all he had learnt and surmised to the AI. It took less than a second.

A test. Morality base evident, came the terse reply.
Threat/warning?
Also.
Obliterate?
Not feasible. Obviously has knowledge of device.
?
Part of the test.
It is disposable then?
As me.

'Yes,' said Cormac, out loud.

Go back, react, returned the silent thought of the AI. Cormac closed his eyes and closed access. Then, abruptly, he departed the Metrotel.

The honour guard remained and Cormac was soon back before Dragon. The dracoman was gone, the cave gone, the head a black silhouette against the red sky.

'Have you seen?' it asked.

'You can destroy Cartis.'

The head turned.

'I mean: *have you seen?*'

Cormac squatted down next to the rucksack he had left.

'Yes,' he said, 'if we are judged and found wanting what happens?'

'You have been judged.'

Cormac waited.

'I have been watching for twenty million of your years. I have seen every sparrow fall.'

'Yes ... that is enough time to come to a conclusion,' said Cormac dryly. He entertained doubts then, about Dragon's sanity.

'You will live,' Dragon said.

Cormac allowed the rigidity to leave him.

'Cartis ... the Monitor ... they were the final push, just to see...' he said, fully understanding now.

'Your AIs are extensions of your own minds as I am an extension of other minds. Had you destroyed me for the few petty threats of this day without regard or understanding of what I truly am every one of your runcibles would have been turned inside out – converted into black holes.'

Cormac reached across and opened his rucksack. From it he took an innocuous looking blue-grey cylinder of metal. With a thought he deactivated it, then he put it away again. A similar, if somewhat larger device, had been used in the system of Cassius to demolish a gas giant.

'Now?' he asked.

'Now, you must leave and I must leave. Your kind will meet mine. My task is done.'

'How will you leave?'

'I will not leave this planet.'

And Cormac knew. He left Dragon, and on his way saw Monitor come and lay down at its side like a faithful dog. Once in the AGC he did not look back.

Lest I be turned into a pillar of salt.

A white sun rose over Aster Colora and hard black shadows were cast, like dice. Cormac later learnt it had been a contra terrene explosion beyond mere human abilities to generate and contain, as it had been contained, in a two kilometre radius.

It was Dragon's last message.

Not a trace of Dragon remained.

ENDS

THE GIRE AND THE BIBRAT

Once upon a time there was a Gire.

Every sound was too loud, every taste, every smell. Every shape seemed as hard-edged and dangerous as broken glass. Fear was the taste of iron in his mouth.

I must triangulate the scream. The only way. I have a sense of direction in this, but a planetary orbit is not enough. Too far. Damn! Only...

He closed his eyes, holding onto the thought.

Three stars at the angles of an isosceles triangle, the two differing sides being twenty-three light years and four point two. Twenty. Three. Light. Years. I'll die. No. I must not think that.

Poised before the twin horns of the runcible, John Tennyson put on the holocorder eye-band. At each stop it would be night and he would look up into the sky. Speed was essential. Should he delay too long between jumps he knew he would not have the will to go on. It had all been calculated. He had a rough idea of the directions and had based his calculations on that.

Galactic North: cold. Hah!

From each runcible he knew the direction to face and the approximate elevation angle. He was ready. All that could let him down now was his mind – his damned oversensitive mind. He stepped forward, his heart racketing in his chest.

I am quince. I am a mitter traveller.

He stepped into the distorting cusp and Skaidon technology flung him, all of him.

STOP.

Mind divided. Mind divided again and again and again. Self-all divided. Infinity slashed down into picoseconds. Thoughts, sub-thoughts, and tenuous connections divided, segmented, sliced, ground down into nothing, bundled into curved space, spread two dimensional to infinity then...

START.

Micro-cosmic dust reassembled. Quarks of love and charm welded. Electrons, protons, and neutrons wound like wool into atoms and atoms stacked into molecules...

He knew that other quince never remembered the scream else they would never travel. He knew that in truth his body was not fragmented, but held in subspace matrices in a place where matter should not exist. But he also knew with his telepathic oh so sensitive mind that he was in Hell. And he remembered. John Tennyson always remembered the near-death: the razor walk.

...complex molecules; proteins, enzymes, aminos; fibre, structure -flashpoint- thought, sub-thought...

Man.

Screaming man.

Once upon a time there was a Bibrat.

He stumbled out under star-pinned night, a scream trying to tear itself from his chest. He suppressed it and searched the sky.

There.

The holocorder threw a frame out from his vision to capture a star system. He turned away, back towards the runcible as it phased in readiness for its next preprogrammed jump. The scream tore from him and he used its fissioning of his thoughts to drive him back.

I must.

He stepped into hell again.

Dante-scream in mind's night.

One step – four point two light years. Another night sky, this one with a moon like a cracked crystal ball hurtling across it, flung away like dreaded futures. He fell to his knees on bluish grass under the glare of arc lamps. He retched, but his stomach had been empty for days.

'Hey, y'alright?'

Subliminally he saw the uniform of a runcible technician. He stood and pushed the man away.

'Suit y'self.'

In the direction he had to look there was only glare. He staggered to an area of plasticrete and gazed upon a mountain range black against a royal purple sky. Like a distortion the moon dropped down behind that blackness and in its wake revealed a star system.

Enough... Return... Twenty... Three...

He turned and his legs were all that contained his will. After hell there was blackness. It was many days before he knew he was home.

Gire: An aerostatic and phototropic fungal mycelium originating somewhere in the second quadrant. It is unusual in that it is trans-stellar and capable of self-levitation and teleport – the only insentient life form capable of this (Some authorities are in disagreement about the meaning of the term 'sentience' in this case. The gire is incapable of the usual forms of sentient communication because it is without extraneous awareness, though it has been proven that its highly complex filament brain is capable of intellection). In appearance the gire is elliptical, though flattened and stretched. Trans-stellar specimens are usually within 10% of the following dimensions: 3m x 1m x .25m. Gordon refers to them as looking like white surf-boards (Refer to 'Sports' subsection 'Earth').

With meticulous care Jennifer Khole removed her lab coat and hung it on the door, then cleaned and dried her hands. A glance around her laboratory confirmed for her that everything was clean and placed precisely where it should be. She smiled ruefully to herself. The care she took with everything had been a source of both ire and amusement at the institute, though no-one had doubted the quality of her work. She looked across at the plaque on the wall above the neutrino scanning nanoscope and nodded to herself. Few researchers could claim to have had recognition from Earth Central. Only to her could be attributed the discovery that the gire, though without awareness of the extraneous, was capable of intellection. Full of self-congratulations she exited her lab. The hand that caught her arm was like a brass claw.

'What the..?'

His face was nothing special and he was shorter than Jennifer. He wore a grey suit with a red pipe-collar shirt. He appeared ordinary in every way but one: his eyes were flat blank metal. Jennifer stared at that flat surface set back from his eyelids – supported flesh crescents. It took her a moment to register what this meant, but when she did she started to shake.

Illegal cyborg!

It was their badge – something intentionally not hidden.

His other grey-gloved hand held up a torque of blue metal.

'Place this around your neck.'

'No!'

His fingers dug into her arm. The pain made her legs go weak and she fell against the door.

'What do you *want?*'

'Place this around your neck or I will break your elbow.'

Jennifer kicked him as hard as she could between his legs. There was no reaction for a moment then he grinned, or grimaced, it was difficult to tell.

'Do not scream or resist. I can render your unconscious and place the collar myself. This will cause delay, but not unacceptable delay.'

He released her arm and held out the collar. Shakily she obeyed.

'You are now wearing a pain inducer.'

Jennifer gasped.

Illegal! Illegal!

'You will obey my instructions precisely.'

He towed her along with him.

'Where are we going? This is *The* Institute... I–'

'We are going to the nearest runcible.'

'This can't be happening.'

'It is,' was the cyborg's flat reply.

Tennyson stepped out onto the balcony and looked down through the shimmer-shield at the city a kilometre below him. The music was so loud now that it was impossible to be heard inside, and he was so drunk that he was nigh incapable of coherent speech. But it did not matter. It did not matter how much he drank, how many people he surrounded himself with, how much he overloaded his senses. He could still hear the mind-scream. Now though he knew where it was coming from. He shuddered and gulped more of his drink.

Screaming man.

'Are you flying?'

'No... I'll... Never again. Drunk.'

She was not listening.

'I imagine it would be like being a sea bird drifting across the surface of an ocean, dipping and sampling the occasional fish. We're all fish to you. You taste us at your leisure.'

She moved up beside him and pressed her breast against

his arm. Together they looked down at the city, it lights spread and lined like dew on some terrible spider's web.

'Do you love me?' she asked.

He slipped into her mind then out as quickly as he could. Hazily he had sampled bitterness, jealousy, and the spores of hate. He fell away from her, out over the city and the murmur and shout. Someone dying. Someone being born. All the voices comfortingly human and easy for him to know or refuse to know. But beyond it all the mind-scream went on and on.

Rippingscreaming.

He realized he had been a diversion for her, not consciously, but there had been no love. Sickened, not by this but by his own lack of strength in the matter of the mind-scream, he turned away without answering and stumbled from the balcony back into the chaos of the party. He knocked a floating vendor aside, spilling a glass of cool-ice psychedelic on the shipfoam floor. He pushed on through the crowd.

...fucking 'path...
...not here not here not here...
...get outa my head...
...I dream...

All the detritus of stoned and drunken minds flowed around him. He tried to ignore thoughts consciously shielded, but his control was awry. He picked up sexual angst and guilty secrets only because they shouted louder as their possessors tried to hide them away.

...I've never had a woman I have I have...
...I lay face-down in the mud and pretended death...

Images of gross sexual acts were thrust at him as if for sale, and one of murder, and one of rape. Mostly though, pathetic inconsequential guilt filled his head. He sloughed them off and pushed on through the crowd. They did not realize that he had known of such things since his adolescence, that because he could delve into other people's minds he could understand them. He was never disgusted or horrified. It was his damnation that he understood, these people at least.

Rippingscreaming.

Out of the party he took a gravchute to the roof-mounted runcible, but he did not use it. Instead he staggered to the iron slug shape of his AGC, fell inside, and instructed it to take him home.

Travel in style.

The thought struck his as hilarious and he laughed until his gorge rose and he threw up on his shoes.

Bibrat: A fungal mycelium originating from the planet Furball in the Gernou system. It is unusual in that its fruiting bodies are a sophisticated sense array and that it is capable of independent movement (This movement is comparable to that of the slime moulds of Earth though considerably faster). It should be noted here that the bibrat, which was jokingly
referred to by Gordon as a 'predatory doormat' (Refer to 'Household Utensils' subsection 'Earth' subsection 'Twentieth Century West') was considered to be no joke by the planetary survey team that landed on Furball (Refer to 'Notable Mistakes' subsection 'Planetary surveys'). Substrata fossil remains date the bibrat at 400 million solstan years in its present form. These remains also tell us that all other forms of life were wiped from Furball at the same time. The bibrat is now cannibalistic and phototropic. Most authorities deny that it is a sentient life form. PSC (Planetary Survey Corps) disagree.

With a hum of nascent agony wrapped round her neck like a venomous reptile, Jennifer could not shake the stupid fear that she might be charged with possession of a proscribed device, but that was only one fear. All her fears allied and rendered her incapable of independent action. Even when the cyborg led her through the crowds of quince at Embarkation she followed meekly. She knew about pain inducers. In fact, the choice of this device to control her was a source of fear in itself. She had been integral in having the device proscribed. But as they approached the two bull's horns containing the shimmering cusp of the runcible field she knew she had to do something. And when to one side she saw the uniforms of two proctors she overcame her fears.

A little pain to buy freedom?

Suddenly she pulled against the clamp on her arm and screamed for help. Her scream was truncated. Red-hot gauze wrapped her skin and someone was sawing through her spine with a blunt knife. Agony locked her in a human crescent. Even so, she saw the proctors coming, and there was hope.

Abruptly the cyborgs free arm was no longer an arm. It was an artifice of glass and glittering metal. A line of black divided vision. The air screamed and the proctors fell vomiting blood. Everyone within a radius of fifty metres fell.

Illegal illegal some part of Jennifer sobbed, then, *I bought death.*

When the pain went away Jennifer cried out them slumped into a hard embrace. The cyborg carried her to the runcible.

Like a discarded child god's building-block the two kilometre cube of cerametal, which *was* Earth Central Security, rested on the shore of Lake Geneva. There were no windows or doors in this structure and for the fifty thousand people that worked there the only ingress was via runcible. They came in naked and left naked, and were scrutinized molecule by molecule each way, yet even they had no idea what information was gathered, what decisions were reached, and what orders given. Each time they left they left part of their minds inside, down-loaded into a mind that knew it all.

Some comedian, at the inception of the project, had christened him Al, but that was now classified information. Al was an A.I., and an exceptionally large A.I. for a time when a planetary co-ordinator could be lost in an ashtray. Al was the size of a tennis ball, but then he processed terabytes of information in his etched-atom circuits in picoseconds – information received, collated, acted upon. Orders given.

Three system jump by known telepath. Sign of distress. Scream report -confirmed.

Kidnap of Jennifer Khole by illegal cyborg. Proscribed weapon used. -Analysis Of Cyclic Rebellion by Edward Landel- ORDER: AGENT 2XG4112039768 ON RUNCIBLE TRACE.

Guard sphere infraction at Furball -confirmed.

Trace to second quadrant. -Terrorism In The Twentieth Century-

ORDER: CANCELLED.

Separatists cause out-phase runcible -confirmed. -Sea Of Death (Hood)-

2.374 Million dead -confirmed.

ORDER: AGENT PRIME CAUSE TO KALIRA.

'What's the problem, Al?'

QUESTION: HOW DO YOU DO THAT?

Laughter.

Rippingscreaming... It always preceded full consciousness. Tennyson jerked awake as he had done every morning for the past six months.

Murder!... No, mind-scream.

It always took him a moment to remember what it was: not the scream of somebody being killed nearby, but the scream of something a distance away impossible for the unaugmented mind to visualize. And it had lasted for those six months.

With a foul taste in his mouth he struggled to get his faculties under control and erect a flimsy mind-stockade. The scream faded almost to inaudibility. His hangover dulled its edge just as the alcohol the night before had. He struggled from his bed and swore blearily. Six months ago he would have searched for his detox and hydration pills. Not now. Now he reached for the bottle of Akvavit on his bedside table and took a swallow.

Pissedhangoveragain.

The garbled thought reached him before the house com told him he had a visitor.

'Come in Kafe,' he said, and the com opened the door.

Kafe, a stocky and dark individual of Asian descent stepped into the apartment and looked at Tennyson speculatively with now-fashionable cat's eyes. Tennyson returned that look and wondered, as always, why Kafe, who sometimes changed his eyes to the dictates of fashion once a month, never had the unsightly birth-mark removed from his cheek. It was a game he played with himself, guessing why. Perhaps one of the reasons he associated with this unpleasant character was because the motivations for much of what Kafe did where buried so deeply in his subconscious mind that even Tennyson had difficulty getting at them. He stared at Kafe and took a defiant swallow of Akvavit.

'You look like shit,' said Kafe.

'Then my appearance is correct.'

'You still hearing it?'

'If hearing is the right word, yes.'

Kafe moved into the room and slumped into one of the loungers. It shifted to accommodate him and he frowned distractedly.

'You have to do something other than that.' He stabbed a finger at the near empty bottle, and Tennyson picked up hints of shady dealings and trading in illegal drugs.

Tennyson nodded. 'I have and I am, though not what you would suggest.'

Kafe raised an eyebrow. 'You haven't been around...'

'I took three jumps. Two of them were about twenty-three light-years.'

'Must've hurt.'

'It took two days of endorphin feed and cerebral stim. I still don't feel right.'

'Why did you do it?'

'Triangulation – to find out where the scream is coming from.'

Raised eyebrow.

'It comes from the Quarrison Drift.'

'Four hundred and eighty light-years. It would kill you.'

'I need help,' said Tennyson, and looked pointedly at his friend. 'Who is there?'

'Only the one, and by the strange workings of coincidence he is here on Kalira.'

'Coincidence,' Tennyson shook his head and took more Akvavit, 'I never believed in it. Tell me about him.'

'Strange character. Very heavy on the mindwork. I came here to tell you about him anyway.'

'May I see?' Empty politeness.

'As you wish...'

Into his mind like a pool, past the angst and badly shielded guilt and to... Horace Blegg.

'A loincloth?'

'Like I said; strange.'

Jennifer soon learnt that obedience was the only way. The other cyborg had stayed behind, probably to die. There was no way it could pass through the runcible carrying proscribed weaponry, and that weaponry was part of it. She had gone through and arrived at her destination with the pain inducer turned to dust around her neck. Waiting for her had been two more cyborgs and another inducer. And now instructions: study this, make a concise report of, predict the probable results of...

In this place.

Through the almost invisible film of her environment suit she studied her surroundings for the nth time, still disbelieving.

The sky was the colour of drying blood cut through with striations of dark green. It seemed not to move at all and was like a carved bowl of heliotrope above her. No moons or stars were in evidence. The land was an endless plate of contorted laval rock from which tentacles of white smoke curled like evil djinns, later to fall as a snow that lay in yellow-brown drifts is rocky crevices. It was a place that would normally have been inaccessible without special authorization and she knew the runcible here must be illegal. Such observations had ceased to matter to her long ago. She turned to look then at her strange companions.

Like the first cyborg they had those blank metal eyes, but with these two their deviation from stock humanity was more than evident, here, where it did not have to be concealed.

The one Jennifer called Speaker, for obvious reasons, had a human face and torso, but that was all. Below its waist (it not being evident if Speaker was male or female) was a transparent sphere, so it appeared as if Speaker floated on a large soap bubble. At the centre of this bubble, hanging like genitalia, was a cluster of unidentifiable hardware. Jennifer had laughed when she had first thought that, but the laughter had not lasted. From Speaker's shoulders sprouted ribbed tentacles which could be plugged into and used to manipulate various devices, such as the antigravity platform they now rode. Attached to the back of Speaker's head was a box twice the size of that head, supported by metal struts running down through its back to the sphere, so it looked as if the flesh part of Speaker was bait threaded onto a hook. From this, various tubes, disks, and needles projected. Jennifer knew a proscribed weapons system when she saw one.

Mute was the most human looking of the two of them and, Jennifer knew, the least human. He walked, had legs, arms, hands, but clinging to the side of his head was something that looked like a giant crystalline slug. The sight of it made Jennifer shudder every time: mental capacity augmented to the level of a planetary AI, pure intellect, emotion suppressed... all well and good if used for good, but in the wrong hands a weapon more potent than a contra-terrene bomb.

To Mute Jennifer attributed her presence here, and the study she was being forced to make, and from which, though only just begun, she was making horrific extrapolations.

'Where is it?' she asked as they drifted over the tortured landscape.

'We will see it soon,' was Speaker's terse reply.

And so they did.

Out of the tentacle smoke drifted the surf-board gire, silent and weird, yet not as perfect as others Jennifer had seen. Across its skin, like the remains of worn fur, clung the attacking body of the bibrat.

At the mouth of the cave greenish snow fell like light motes down a silk curtain. In his survival suit Tennyson was warm, though he could not see how Blegg kept from shivering. The old man sat Buddha-like on the wet stone with only a leather pouch to support his genitals.

'What is required is a total alteration of your mindset. You realize, that after this alteration, your need to seek out the source of this scream will be eliminated?'

Tennyson nodded, grasping that immediately. He had tried to read the old man earlier and had come up against the most effective shield he had ever encountered. It had been like slamming head-first into a granite wall. But Tennyson, who was noted for his pigheadedness, had to try again.

Nothingness.

Vast empty... void void void...

He was expanding, coming apart. Suddenly there was red fire all around him and through him. He screamed.

Void.

'What is required is a total alteration of your mindset...'

Flat on his back on the floor of the cave Tennyson shivered. He then reached to the sore split on the back of his head. His fingers came away red-dipped.

'What the Hell?' he sat upright. Before him Blegg was floating a metre off of the stone floor.

'Hell indeed if you trespass. Thou shalt not.'

'Huh?'

'You understand?'

Tennyson nodded woodenly. 'What is this alteration?'

'To survive the experience of the Skaidon warp and retain your powers you must understand it fully, be able to create it inside you, and to do this you must become pure intellection. You must subordinate your survival instincts. Total mind instinct inversion. You have sampled what that means... Thou understands?'

'Loss of humanity?'

'Apotheosis, but define humanity.'

'Your mind... you are not human.'

'You have not defined humanity. A stone is not human. You have merely told me that a human is not a stone.'

'Cut the philosophical crap!'

Blegg settled to the floor of the cave and turned his wrinkled slant-eyed visage to one side.

'Everything I say has relevance. Stones. Do you know what a philosopher's stone is?'

'No.'

'It is a stone said to have the property of being able to transmute base metals into gold. It was much sought after by alchemists.'

'Gold is cheap.'

'Yes, but it has properties other metals lack. It corrodes very little, is highly malleable and conductive. I, should you wish it, will be your philosopher's stone.'

Now, as Blegg turned to meet his stare, Tennyson felt panic. At once the cave seemed too small.

Apotheosis? Godhood?

'What are you?' he asked, his voice catching in his throat.

'You know my name.'

'I touched your mind and it was like fire. You look like a man but you're not human.'

'Thou may trespass, John Tennyson.'

'I'm scared of you.'

'You're scared to become like me, infant. It is time for you to grow up, time for you to know thyself.'

'I don't know who you are, that is certain.'

'I am the first. I came to know myself in a burning city

longer ago than I care to remember. I am Horace Blegg, but I had a different name when the Enola Gay flew over my home city of Hiroshima. I came to know myself in fire, and that fire I hold for others. Come into my fire, John Tennyson.'

Fire reached for him, and though fearing, he accepted it. And he screamed on the forge of the gods.

Purity and inner vision, cellular awareness: cut, I bleed.

Blegg sat before him with an enigmatic smile on his face.

Pain from the cut comes here. I know the cut. Pain is superfluous. Remove it from life-image. Once pain. Once cut. Gone.

Tennyson reached to the back of his head and felt a lump of scar-tissue dissolving under his fingertips.

'I am human.'

'Yes...'

'Why are you old?'

'Respectability,' said Blegg, then he raised his arms and the wrinkles and flaccid skin filled. In moments a youth sat before Tennyson.

'Thou understands?'

Tennyson nodded.

'Now listen to the mind-scream.'

Tennyson did so, automatically separating himself from the pain of it. 'It's the pain of birth,' he said wonderingly.

'Yes...'

'I will go to it. I am needed.'

Blegg allowed himself a wry grin. 'You were called, mind-smith, midwife.'

Tennyson looked at him sharply. 'I was called. Why not you?'

'I initiate, thus I am sometimes called Prime Cause. I was

sent here by Earth Central, but I am also integral to Earth Central.'

'Too valuable to risk.'

Blegg grinned. 'Do not let this make you feel inferior. You are now more important than you were.'

'One human being more important than another?'

'I think so. Oppenhiemer was very important in his time, more important than Hitler.'

'I'm not sure I believe your story, old man.'

'That is not important.'

'Tell me what is then.'

'The scream you hear. Look into my mind and I will show you two life forms, what you must do, how you must accomplish it, and how you can survive.'

Warily Tennyson sank into Blegg's mind. No fire this time, but a pool – ripples and eddies of thought.

'I see, but the cyborgs?'

'Have you learnt nothing?'

'Ah, a contra-terrene device in the human one. What about the girl? No need to ask. I can protect her. Perhaps your stories are true old man. The gire? The bibrat?'

'Will be one. Their battle, their fusion, and their birth will go beyond the physical.'

'Then all that remains is the journey.'

With a sick clenching of her stomach Jennifer remembered the finishing words of a certain professor's speech at a conference she had attended on Calisto. The speech had been about extra-terrestrial fungal life forms.

'We can draw few conclusions when taking into account the conflicting reports of the PSC and such dubious authorities as Gordon, and those conclusions only where the reports concur.

One conclusion I'm sure you will agree with is that Earth Central's enclosure of Furball was necessary. Should a bibrat colony, or rather, infestation, become established on any inhabited world that world would have to be abandoned.'

At this point the professor, a young man noted for his radical views, had paused, and Jennifer had known what was going to hit the fan.

'One can only question Earth Central's wisdom as to its reluctance to utterly obliterate furball.'

There had been uproar. Jennifer remembered it with a twisting of her mouth that did not quite make it to a smile as tears trickled from her eyes. She rested her head on the console before her.

Every moment of delay is another of life. But what is my life at the moment?

She pushed away from the console and began typing in her final analysis. It would be confirmed with her psych-print, and she knew it would not be used as a scientific paper, but as a threat.

Conclusions as to survivability:

Though the bibrat is attacking the gire as earth type mycelia attack rotting vegetation and their perpetual enemies the nematodes i.e. it is feeding on the gire, the gire is reacting on the same microscopic level with its autoimmune defense. In effect they are feeding on each other. For most fungal life forms this could only be seen as a process of attrition – the one with the greater body mass being the survivor, should it be able to sustain the damage done to it.

Why can't I lie? Perfection? No, Mute would know.

In this case the rules are different. The gire has greater body mass, the bibrat higher resilience, and both are phototropic. Over a period of one solstan month I have detected no imbalance...

Jennifer held a picture in her mind: a thousand, a million, more, gires spreading from hidden locations across the galaxy, teleporting, drifting undetected down onto inhabited worlds, bibrat riders sporulating... All infected: gires, worlds.

...I can only assume that this... symbiosis, no, mutual parasitism... would exist long enough for the gire to go trans-stellar and beyond...

She continued, adding foot-notes and various proofs of her observations. She was a perfectionist, and it was obvious what they had here: a weapon like none ever before known. She did not, however, get a chance to complete the work. Suddenly the grav-platform lurched and hurtled up into the heliotrope sky. Jennifer was thrown to the metal deck.

No, not now! I want to live! was her only thought as the G-forces drove the breath from her body.

In the distort shimmer-place one thought: *Once pain, no pain, gone.*

Coming out of the warp he let the scream flow through him just as he observed that other nascent scream flow and die. His mind had appeared to come apart but, *all* of his mind had encompassed it. And he stepped from once-hell to hellscape.

Here.

He let his mind slide into red and green night then fall on the inchoate being.

Two screams: both think, both feel.

He looked through the underspace he now knew so intimately and saw the two primitively telepathic intelligences tearing at each other as did their bodies. He pushed them to fusion and the screaming stopped.

Other?

He linked confusion and it cancelled.
Other?
He tore at the strands of the physical and wove them. The gire gained the sensorium of the bibrat and the bibrat the intellect of the gire.
Other! Other!
The surf-board shape lurched from its drifting flight. Strands began to break.
OO-tt-hh-ee-rr!!
Now.
Tennyson broke away and looked up from his crouched position in the shadow of a rock shaped like a witch frozen in hellish dance. A grav-platform was falling towards him like a giant coin. White light strobed the landscape and rock turned molten. But Tennyson had stepped away – half a kilometre away. From there he clawed at the platform and at Speaker's mind.

Gasping for breath Jennifer tried to pull herself upright. A wind was howling across the platform and it tilted to the horizon. She heard Speaker's strained voice; 'Someone controlling... Someone... Destruct.' Then a hand of force snatched her away.

Mute's digital cry went, *No no no no no no.*

Distantly a surf-board shape fell to the ground as an electric sun lit its horizon.

OTHER!!

Blue-white fire wrapped around the planet like a closing eyelid and a disc of fire cut it. With the seeming slowness of a leviathan it began to spin itself to plasma and small fragments of heavy metal. Out of this chaos a bright mind rode the shock-flash, surfing on light into the void. In a fold in space two thoughts followed it out.

I want to live.
And an ironic thought: *So you survived Hiroshima, old man.*

ENDS

WALKING JOHN AND BIRD

I grace Bird with gender yet I still do not know if she is a living creature or a machine. She has the disquieting beauty of something as perfectly functional as a honed blade, her body-shape that of an Arctic tern fashioned, or grown, of mirror-bright metal as jointless as mercury. Her head is an elongated teardrop and her beak, if such it could be called, never opens. In my darker moments I entertain the notion that, should it open, the sound to issue forth will be my death knell. But I wax too lyrical. Killing is a function she performs so very well.

When she is visible people mistakenly believe Bird has the fragility of her namesakes. The experts who probed and tested her learnt to their consternation she was impervious to any scan, any radiation. Neutrons bounce off her surface as readily as bullets. That I discovered, as did some people who had wanted to learn her secrets and who had been prepared to use any means. Past now, and those people dead. They had threatened my life and paid the penalty. But the mystery remained.

I cannot remember the name of the world, but then I am a traveller and the names of worlds slip by me as readily as the names of the people I meet. It is a dark place where green grass and oak trees grow, and had recently been opened for colonization after terraforming. What mostly distinguishes it in my recollection is a cracked crystal ball of a moon hurtling across the sky like a bubble across molten glass, and a conversation:

'Mystery! Hah!'

The old man had paused then and squinted speculatively up at Bird. After a moment he scratched his grey beard and continued.

'Yes, I suppose you're right. It's just I can't take you seriously. I've spent a century and a half trying to resolve some ... mysteries, and I'm no closer. Your protest strikes me as feeble.'

'You do not walk with death at your shoulder,' I told him.

The old man bent down with the hose he was holding and began to vacuum dust out of the excavation.

'Don't be so conceited. We all do.'

'It does not have the same immediacy,' I told him, feeling rather foolish. He shrugged and continued vacuuming for a while before saying anything more.

'There was one who answered questions for me that none of Earth's AIs could answer.'

'Yes?'

'Dragon. Speak to Dragon. But be careful. The answer sometimes given is like that which hovers at your shoulder.'

Now I stood before a runcible, the device invented by Skaidon Iversus, in conjunction with an AI, that made instantaneous travel a reality. Thus I was quince: a mitter traveller. And I was on my way to see a creature reputedly older than human history and apparently the size of a mountain. Bird was with me of course, a few metres above my head, and when I stepped between those twin bull's horns into the space-twisting cusp, she followed, but by her own methods. I know not how.

Space and time ceased to exist for ... yet there was no time so it could not have been for an instant too subliminal to register. One world blinked out and another blinked into existence. I found myself gazing across a landscape of pink and black rock below a metallic red sky. This was Aster Colora, the fabled world of Dragon. I tasted salt in the air and the taint of scrap yards. Bird was with me.

The only city on Aster Colora was called Cartis. I rented an AGC at the runcible facility and headed that way, Bird fading into invisibility at my behest. It is a one-sided communication we have. Bird reacts to my emotions. How well I know she reacts to my fear. I could still see her hovering like a holographic icon, but by her translucence I knew she was invisible to others.

    Once in the AGC I put its computer on line and instructed it to take me to a decent hotel. It informed me that there was only one, so I told it to take me there. It lifted from the ground with a slight rumbling sound. I had noticed that much of the equipment round the runcible facility was somewhat decrepit. This was how things got this far from Earth. Once in the air the car accelerated with a lurch and specks of pink snow slid from the frictionless screen. I contemplated then what I must do.

    I had to speak to Dragon, which for most people is an uncomplicated affair. All they had to do was address Dragon's com' unit through one of the local AIs. I, on the other hand, did not want anyone to know I was here, for I knew that as soon as my identity was registered on the net there would be certain people who would pick it up – people I had no wish to speak with. The price of fame.

The Metrotel was not such a bad place. I was soon in a comfortable room on the top floor ordering myself a meal and talking to hotel's AI.

'I want a complete lock on my identity while I am here. I do not want any visitors.'

'Lock enabled,' a woman's voice told me. 'But there may have been information leakage when you were booking in. Should anyone visit I will deny that you are present.'

'Thank you. Now, I am hungry. Do you have a menu?'

'Yes, John. I would recommend the Scylla crab with croquette potatoes and buttered hinch-carrots...'

The menu was running down the screen as she spoke and I was surprised at some of the things being shown there. I made my selection

'Steak, chips and peas and a couple of litres of IPA.'

It was ersatz Earth, but I was mature enough to admit I could not tell the difference. It was also expensive, but what the hell, you only live once...

Two days of work proved to me there was no way round getting my identity registered if I wanted to talk to Dragon. I considered going to the creature in person, but the area all around was heavily monitored to prevent joy riders testing the two kilometre radius. Dragon, it seemed, had made a rule that no machinery bigger than a man was to get closer than two kilometres. I was told that there was ring of smashed AGCs and AG scooters at that limit. This was Dragon's world and Cartis only had colony status. It was with reluctance that I registered as a petitioner and awaited my slot. The expected call was not long in coming.

'I can no longer deny your presence here,' the hotel AI informed me. 'There is a Dawn Keltree here to see you.'

'Tell her I am not seeing anyone.'

I sat back in my chair and returned my concentration to the screen once the interrupt had passed. The lecture was being given by a Professor Darson.

'The creature we know as Dragon consists of four conjoined spheres each a kilometre across. The primary analysis of Dragon material brought the conclusion that it is silicon based, but there are anomalies—'

I clicked back to another lecture by the same man, but retained the pictures of Dragon. There it was: the spheres, here wreathed in cloud, then a separate cut-out screen showing pseudopodia, like giant one-eyed cobras, junking an AGC that had crossed the boundary. A subscript quickly outlined the story of students getting through security for a prank. Their bodies were reportedly still in the AGC as no one could be bothered to retrieve them without transport. Darson droned on.

'—was not the name given but the name claimed. So why did it name itself after a creature of myth? Gordon has it that—'

'Sorry to interrupt again. Ms Keltree has left a message. Do you wish to view it?'

'Go on then. This is getting boring. Darson comes out with nothing but speculation.'

Ms Keltree was very pretty, in an overly athletic way, and very anxious.

'This is Dawn Keltree of The Cartis Observer. Now ... I know you are pursued by the press wherever you arrive, but perhaps we can be of some assistance to you ... I see that you have registered as a petitioner. Well ... we have information about Dragon in our files you won't find on the standard net. Interested? If you are, just get the hotel AI to contact me. I'll be right round.'

I chuckled at her nerve. She was obviously new to the game and in hot pursuit of her big break. I then considered taking her up on her offer. What had I got to lose? I could not prevent them putting out some story about me just as I could not prevent it being known I was here. What I could do was influence the story in some way and make some money out of it.

'AI, put me through to Ms Keltree if you can.'

Instantly her face flickered back onto the screen.

'The McCaffrey at seven o'clock. You're buying.'

Her face became one big grin, but before she could say anything more I turned off the screen with the manual control. Let her say it all tonight. I would listen, answer questions, charge a suitable fee.

The McCaffrey is one of those very expensive places that specialize in personal service and handmade foods. As I stepped through the door I noted one or two diners look at me with a deep fascination then pretend nonchalance as they once again concentrated on their food. Obviously word got around. Ms Keltree rose from her seat to greet me and I discovered something about her that her screen image had not shown: she was very tall.

'I am glad you could spare the time,' she said as she shook my hand.

'My time is at a premium.'

'Of course ... a percentage ...?'

She seemed at a loss. I sat down.

'A flat payment of one hundred Solars. Is that agreeable?'

I picked up the menu and opened it. For a moment I thought it was real paper, but the set meals scrolled as a ran my finger up the side. I looked up and waited for her to take her seat. Perhaps my mercenary attitude had confused her ... no, I realised she must be on a direct link with her employers as she touched her fingertips below her ears and frowned.

'Yes, that is acceptable.' She sat down.

I reached out and touched the privacy touchplate at the centre of the table and the sounds of conversation died around us.

'You may begin,' I said, interlacing my fingers before me.

She studied me for a long moment.

'Is Bird here with you?'

I glanced up to my left to where Bird held station below the crystal lights.

'Bird is always with me.'

She looked up as well and Bird slid into visible solidity then out of it again. Ms Keltree stared in fascination then turned back to me when Bird was gone.

'Are you any closer to knowing what it is?'

'Perhaps. I am here to ask your Dragon what I might ...'

I told her then about the archaeologist and about my recent travels, of the bird religion of the Knastil, the ancient writings of Baraluck, how none of these had yielded the information I sought. We ordered a meal of baked Scylla crabs and sugar bread and drank a couple of bottles of Chianti. I found I enjoyed speaking to her, even if much of what I said had been practised on other worlds. Near the end of the meal she came to the questions to which I knew no answer.

'You say you have been travelling with Bird for fifty years, yet I have found references to "Walking John and Bird" from as long ago as three centuries Solstan.'

'Yes, I've heard that before, but I can assure you it has only been fifty years. I can only ascribe those legends to hearsay.'

'Could it be that Bird travelled with someone else?'

The thought had never occurred to me. I sat back and sipped my wine.

'That might be worth looking into,' I said, grudgingly.

She nodded then turned aside as a floating vendor offered her a post prandial selection. She took mint chocolates. I took a cigar because I was feeling pompous.

'Another aspect of your relationship I am curious about is the empathy ... or telepathy. Have you ever consulted with a telepath?'

'Sorry?'

'Bird reacts to your emotions. There is some kind of mental link. I would have thought a good telepath might be able to learn something from this.'

I shook my head. She was walking into fantasy land now.

'I am sure a good telepath would be most useful, if there were such a thing.'

'There is John Tennyson of Earth and Horace Blegg.'

'Horace Blegg is a legend and I have never heard of this Tennyson.'

She nodded solemnly.

'Yes, legends ... Until this morning I would have said the same about you.'

I returned to my Hotel in a bemused mood and it was only as I entered the lobby that I noticed the man who had been following me. He slid into the shadows when I turned towards him though, and was soon gone. I forgot about him.

Dragon refused to speak to me in any sensible manner. I spent a frustrating morning putting questions through my comlink and getting Delphic and sometimes silly replies.

'I am known as Walking John, inevitable really, as I am a traveller and my real name is John Walker ... With me is the entity known simply as Bird. Do you know anything of this entity?'

'Birds have a wonderful sense of direction.'

A humourless statement of fact.

'You are reputedly aware of much that occurs in the human world. You must have known of my arrival here. I was directed here by the archaeologist Sendel Dyne who once asked you questions no AI could answer. He said you might have answers for me. Please, what do you know of Bird?'

'Digging in the dust for facts about dust.'

And so, and thus. It was almost as if I were hooked up to random sentence generator that picked up on a single fact in a spoken sentence and generated another sentence from it. I received no answers from Dragon. The frustration drove me to a bottle of whisky at midday and I was feeling somewhat lugubrious when I received Ms Keltree's second call. She was not slow in getting to the point.

'We have information as to the location of Horace Blegg.'

'That is very interesting,' I said with as much lack of interest as I could muster. I was, of course, hooked. 'How did you come by this information?'

'It was recently uncovered by one of our permanent search programmes.'

'How recently?'

She paused significantly before replying.

'Last night.'

The long arm of coincidence. Yeah.

'May I come and discuss this with you? We have an offer we would like to make.'

'Let's make it the McCaffrey at seven. I am rather busy at present.'

'Okay, see you there.'
I had lied of course. I had absolutely nothing to do. I had used up my com time with Dragon and was pissed, in both senses of the word. What I really wanted was not to appear to be too eager, and have time to sober up.

It took ten minutes with two capsules and a pint of orange juice to sober me up and after that I was wandering around my apartment trying to come to a decision about what I was to do next. Often I stopped and stared at Bird in the hope that inspiration would come from that source. A foolish hope for it never had. For me, most of the time, Bird was merely present.

Another fifty minutes dragged past while I showered and changed in readiness for my jaunt to the McCaffrey. When I eventually left it was with a degree of eagerness. Things were happening, I felt. I would soon learning something. It never occurred to me then that I might learn things I did not want to know.

Ms Keltree was not there before me this time so I took a table and ordered a carafe of blue wine. The drink, though potent, did little for me, following as it did on the two Soberups I'd taken. Ms Keltree turned up when I was on my second glass and beginning to feel agitated.

'I'm sorry, so sorry to keep you waiting,' she said, and seated herself with artless flirtation in her tight and revealing clothing in an attempt to defuse any anger I might feel. My anger was dissipated, not because of any sexual attraction I felt, but because the naivety of her actions was appealing. We ordered the special of the day, which was a selection of Asiatic curries, and she immediately came across with the sell.

'As I told you we know where Horace Blegg is presently located,' she told me as she thrust her cleavage in my general direction.

'And this you consider to be of interest to me?'

'Oh yes.'

'If I recollect aright the idea of a telepath being able to tell me something new about Bird came from you. As it happens I still do not believe such a creature exists.'

'He exists and I feel certain it would be to your advantage to meet him.'

'Yes, but how is it to *your* advantage?'

She sat back then, crossed her legs in a different direction, and shook her hair about her shoulders. I nearly burst out laughing.

'In exchange for the location of Horace Blegg we would like all rights to the story and to have a reporter with you at the moment of the encounter.'

'You, presumably?'

She smiled. 'Yes, me.'

The meal arrived then at that suitable juncture and we ate in silence for a short time.

'This could of course just be a ploy to get a reporter with me for a long period of time. I would have to check the validity of your information before agreeing.'

She gave me dumb blond expression of surprise number one. This was beginning to irritate me – her attitude and the acid stomach I'd acquired from my boozing earlier.

'I also have not finished my researches here. I was considering taking on more com time with Dragon. I find its evasiveness intriguing.'

All of a sudden Ms Keltree snapped out of her pretend daze, perhaps at the realisation that the sex-slanted ploy might not work.

'Would you agree to a contract ... on the validation of our information?'

'I don't know that your information would be worth my trouble. Runcible jaunts are not so cheap.'

'We are prepared to offer a thousand Solars block payment to assist things along. This way nobody loses. We get a story, and if you do not get information on Bird you will at least have the money for much more com time with Dragon when you return.'

This was more like it. My digestion improved immeasurably.

'Okay, I presume this conversation is being recorded.'
'Under seal.'
'Then I agree. When do we go, and where do we go?'

Ms Keltree had difficulty suppressing the smug look of victory from her face and I turned from her to allow her a moment to get herself under control. At that moment my gaze strayed to a nearby table where a man sat alone with an untouched meal on a plate before him. He was staring at me intently. I let my gaze stray past him and brought my attention back Ms Keltree. I knew that man, but I could not remember from where.

'If it is agreeable to you we will leave early tomorrow morning. If I may I will join you at your roofport and we'll take an AGC to the Runcible at about eight. Is that all right?'

'Fine,' I said, still distracted by the familiar face. Ms Keltree then told me where we were going and all my attention returned to her. There, that place, full circle.

We talked a while longer and it was with a kind of inevitability I felt that we ended up in my hotel room for another drink or two. When Ms Keltree asked me if I would like to have sex with her I said 'yes' immediately, my decision having been made on an unconscious level before I consciously knew about it. This is often the case with me. I did not then know why.

I confirmed that Horace Blegg was reported by the runcible AI of Thurvis to be present on that world, this through time bought from my hotel AI. There was no other information about him; why he was there, how long he would be there, and where exactly on that world he was. The time when this information became available and the place it became available from put breaking strain on the long arm of coincidence.

The morning air was chill and specks of reddish snow were blown here and there and melted on the skin to form droplets like blood. Looking at my bare arm it appeared to me that my skin had been worked over with needles. Dawn swore about the red specks evenly speckling her skin-tight white trousers.

'What is it?' I asked.

'Bloody snow!' she said, which seemed apposite. She then went on to explain that this colouring was caused by a mixture of dust and iron salts blown up into the air and mixed with the heavily peroxided water. The result was similar to being spattered with blood. The stuff turned brown as it dried out.

The AGC was in better condition than the one I arrived in and turned out to be one belonging to the Cartis observer. Once we were seated inside the vehicle and it was airborne Dawn removed a small cleaning device and ran it over her trousers. That such a device was in the AGC showed this snow was common.

At the runcible station there was no wait. We went directly to this open air runcible and after keying and palming to confirm our destination we stepped through one after the other into the huge lobby at Thurvis and a chaos of crowds.

'We just made it,' Dawn told me as we fought our way to the exit. She pointed to the announcement board. The runcible had gone into one way operation to prevent dangerous overcrowding. People could now only leave Thurvis, they could not arrive. All over the runcible network people bound for Thurvis would be stepping through the Skaidon cusp to be stored in no-space, basically ceasing to exist, for a while.

'I wonder what all this is about?' I asked.

'Horace Blegg,' she told me, and only then did I notice the amount of recording equipment there was in the lobby. Like a swarm of huge silver bees holocorders hovered in the air. I noted with interest how some of them became confused when Bird, though not visible in the human spectrum, floated past or through them. On the floor scent recorders and all manner of analysers scuttled about on metal insect legs, or squealed about on fat little tyres. Hover luggage weaved in and out of this crowd like pets seeking owners, which was much the case.

''lo Dawn!'

'Nice to see you Dawn!'

'Ms Keltree!'

Dawn nodded and smiled to fellow professionals, but I could see she looked very worried. Perhaps she was thinking it very unlikely we would be able to get to see Horace Blegg. I was not so sure there would be a problem. Once we were free of the lobby and out in the open where the crowds were being thinned by the AG taxis, she called up the local AI on a console inset into a rock in the shade of a huge oak tree.

'Could you give me the present location of Horace Blegg?'

'Thurvis.'

'Could you be more specific?'

'No.'

I took hold of her arm.

'There are people I can try. I have contacts.'

'Yes,' I said, 'but first we have somewhere to go. Call up a taxi.'

The taxi took a while to arrive as obviously the local service was under some pressure transporting the press of many worlds to the capital city of this one. When I told it where I wanted to go I am sure I evinced surprise from the on board computer. It took us anyway.

Thurvis: recently opened for colonization after terraforming, but only certain areas. It was a place of immense forests and heaths. It was a park world. But there were also a few places kept deliberately bare of life, places where the ancient remains of a civilization already fallen into ruin when humans had not decided which direction to take: back into the sea or out onto the plains of Africa. The AGC landed us in the same place as it had landed me only a few weeks before. As I climbed out I could hear the vacuum cleaner running in the excavation. The old man was there, carefully uncovering the shape of a wall in the earth and the few artefacts to survive. He looked up as we approached.

'Horace Blegg I presume,' I said.

He grinned wickedly.

'I sent you to Dragon because Dragon will have the answers.'

I nodded, sipped at the glass of whisky he had provided me with, and slowly studied the interior of his tent. Dawn, sitting on a cerametal box marked 'Artefact, Do Not Transmit' was in her idea of heaven now she was over the initial shock. Around her, in the air and on the ground, was a formidable array of recording equipment. She was even writing in a paper pad.

'Dragon was uncooperative,' I told him.

'You should not have used the com. You should have walked directly to Dragon.'

I nodded with cool assurance as if I had considered this. In reality the thought had never occurred to me. Blegg went on.

'I feel Dragon fears Bird. I would like to know why.'

'So would I, if that is the case, but I am here now and I would like to know what you can tell me, and what your interest is.'

Blegg studied me with eyes like lead shot and I knew with a certainty that behind those eyes was a millstone of a mind that ground very small indeed. Something about this man exhilarated me, frightened me.

'First, my interest: I am agent Prime Cause and I work for Earth Central. Anything that might affect the stability of the human civilization is of interest to me. Bird is an unknown with unknown capabilities. As to what I know ... I can tell you there is a subspace link between you and Bird that has a physical integrity. It is almost matter yet it is in the realm of the psyche.'

'What might that mean?'

'It probably means that Bird is part of you, an extension of you, but I know little beyond that without a probe.'

I felt the danger then, but my need to know was stronger.

'Probe me then.'

'It could kill you.'

'You also,' I glanced over my shoulder to where Bird, now visible, turned slowly in the air like a string hung ornament. As I turned back to Blegg he suddenly seemed to be miles away from me. Abruptly I felt an abyss opening round me, then Blegg was before me again.

'First, this.'

He held in his hand a small pistol that seemed made of the most delicate chalky shell and weighed almost nothing.

'Why? What do I need this for?'

'It is there for need. You will know.'

I peered at the pistol in my hand. It was like a toy, and it faded out of existence as I looked at it. I knew then I was in some kind of dream space. I glanced round at Dawn and she looked blank, mindless.

'Now,' said Blegg, and the abyss was full of fire. I might have screamed then, I do not know if it was me or Blegg. I heard the vicious drone of Bird as I had once heard it before. I think I warned him, for Blegg went flat as a picture, turned into a line, and disappeared a microsecond before Bird passed through where he was.

'Okay, you're okay now.'

Dawn was holding my head against her breast and rocking me. I cannot remember what happened between this moment and the disappearance of Blegg. I breathed easy and pulled my head away. Her shirt was soaked with blood. I checked my face and head for wounds.

'Your nose bled, and you were crying it.'

A little unsteadily I reached for Blegg's bottle of whisky and not bothering with a glass I drained a fair bit of it.

'Let's get back to Dragon territory. You got enough for a story?'

'More than. Too much.'

I doubted it, oh I doubted it once a few effects had worn away. I stood up, capped Blegg's bottle, and stood it next to something he had been cleaning on a portable table. It looked like a small ceramic gun, and that reminded me of the gun he had given me, or not given me. I felt a pressure, light as a fly, at the centre of the palm of my hand. I did not believe it, and anyway, runcible proscription never let weapons through. I turned away, leaving the bottle for him, for I suspected he would be back for it. It was good whisky.

The runcible facility had cleared fairly much by the time we reached it – we learnt to our surprise we had been gone for eleven solstan hours – though we got some strange looks from a few individuals as we walked across the lobby. I had blood crusted on my face and Dawn, what with my blood and the spattering from the red snow of Aster Colora, appeared to have been taking a bath in it. Before heading for the runcible, we stopped and enquired at a console.

'Could you tell me the present location of Horace Blegg?' I asked.

'Who's asking?' The question shot back immediately, and I knew I was talking directly to the Runcible AI and not one of its subminds.

'John Walker.'

'Blegg is quite safe and will be in contact with you again after you return to Aster Colora.'

Fine.

We headed for the runcible.

Stepping from the cool outdoor runcible on Aster Colora I felt exhaustion come down on me like a lead sheet. Looking to

Dawn I saw that she felt much the same. We slouched to the only AGC in the area and climbed inside with a feeling of relief.

'I want a shower, some brandy, and a sleep,' said Dawn.

I nodded and after pushing in my credit card I spoke into the AGC's computer, 'AGC, take us to the metrotel.' Obligingly it lifted into the air. I lay back and closed my eyes.

'What happened when Blegg probed you? Why did Bird attack him?'

'It decided he was attacking me in some way.'

'And always reacts so to a threat to you?'

'Always.'

I drifted for a moment then until she brought me back with another question.

'What about indirect threats?'

'I don't know. Nothing, I think. Only direct threats to my life. There has only been one other occasion.'

'Yes, I know about that. Someone kidnapped you and tried to get information from you about Bird.'

'They used drugs and VR first and when that did not work they tried pain. That is when Bird reacted. She killed three men and two women in about a second. Two of them were cyborgs. They were all Separatists.'

There was a long silence then before Dawn spoke again. I had almost drifted off to sleep.

'This AGC isn't taking us to Cartis.'

Suddenly I was very awake. In that instant two facts became very clear to me. The man in the McCaffrey was one of the Separatists who had not been present when his fellows had decided to use torture. And I had been with Bird for more than the fifty years I had supposed and more than the three centuries Dawn Keltree had suggested.

The AGC fled on the red sunrise of another day, not that the sun could be seen. Dawn tried all her communications equipment to no avail. I tried the one in my wristwatch and only got static. The solstan time-setting broadcast by the runcible AI had also been interrupted. I glanced behind the AGC and Bird was there as solid as a heat-seeking missile.

'Try the panel ... Manual control.' Dawn sounded panicky, which surprised me. I carefully pulled at the fastenings to the control panel and found them locked solid. I took hold of the joystick and found it also was locked in place.

'Oh for fucksake!'

Dawn smashed her nigh indestructible holocorder against the panel and tried to pull open the casing from the split she had made. A small red lightning flung her back in her seat and filled the inside of the AGC with the smell of burning hair.

'You all right?'

She nodded, but she was shaking badly.

'That wasn't from the console,' she said.

'I know,' I said. I recognised the red lightning from somewhere. Where? Oh yes, a place called Tantalus III now, static discharge projected through subspace, the weapon that brought an empire down. I was cold, emotionless, until I realised that the empire I had been thinking about had not been a human empire, had not in fact been of any race I should have known ... I got the horrors then.

The AGC came into land as Dawn recovered her composure and made sure all her recording devices were operating. We landed in conditions of fine sleet and would have stayed in the AGC if the door had not opened and a threatening flicker of red fire come into existence beside us. Dawn got out first with her recording devices moving out ahead of her like faithful sheep dogs. As I stepped out there was a sound like a metal wall being hit with a hammer and all her devices ceased to function. The holocorder fell out of the air.

'What the hell is this?'

'Separatists I think.'

'But where?'

I shrugged. There was no one about. We moved out into the wasteland as the AGC lifted into the air behind us and headed back to Cartis. Was that it then? We weren't going back. They would be more prepared this time. Something would happen. Something. The ground shook then and fifty metres ahead of us something broke through and rose into the air. I recognised the giant cobra shape immediately, as did Dawn.

'Dragon, then,' I said.

It rose ten metres into the air, another rose beside it, then another on the other side. Eyes like blue crystal observed us from where a cobra's mouths would have been. I took a step forward, then hesitated. There was something else. Had it risen to the surface also? Between myself and these fleshy extrusions of Dragon – they reached for many kilometres under the ground so the tapes told me – lay something else, a black shape, almost like a coffin, only streamlined and somehow sinister.

'What, is that?'

I had no reply for her. The shape rose into the air, something rippled across its surface and a circle of ground underneath it became molten. I stepped back and Bird was in front of me in a shimmering curtain that bowed under the pressure of some force from the black object. A terrible screaming filled the air. Dawn clapped her hands over her ears and fell to the ground. I felt my eardrums burst and liquid running down my neck. The pain did not hit me until the shimmering curtain broke and Bird and the black object met with a thunderclap, then I too fell to the ground and clasped my hands over my bleeding ears.

    The storm did not abate, it moved away. The ground shook and the sky filled with flashes of light I quickly turned my eyes from. Even then the vision out of my right eye seemed charred. This was the kind of light that would do to a retina what that sound had done to my eardrums. Dawn was up onto her knees next to me. She said something, but all I got was a dull mumbling. I shook my head and wished I had not. The lights in the distance dimmed a little and I dared a quick glimpse. A flicker of something, like a gull picked out by sunlight against tearing cloud, and its shadow, black. So much nearer the three cobra heads were watching, perhaps immune to the light that had burnt the vision of my right eye. I gestured to Dawn and we both turned away from the battle and those distant dangerous lights, right into a closer danger.

    Fifty years ago the Separatists had tried for the technology Bird represented. Two of them had been cyborgs, illegal cyborgs, because they were part man and part proscribed weaponry. One of them had been much like this one. Half a man, the torso, perched on a translucent sphere inside which, like metalled guts, hung and array of devices. From where the arms should have been projected segmented tentacles, three from each shoulder, each ending in a different tool or weapon. Behind and curved round the distended and surgery scarred head was a metal box like a bloated horse shoe. From this metal struts went down through its back into the sphere. It was floating about a metre off the ground. And it had come for me. I glanced at Dawn just as she was saying something to the cyborg. She was smiling as she stepped to one side to retrieve her holocorder. Her expression did not have time to change before the cyborg blew her spine and part of her ribcage out of her back.

I think Blegg had expected something like this, or had he just assumed I would kill? The pressure against the palm of my hand was still the same as I lifted that hand, pointed the gun at the cyborg and pulled back on a trigger I thought I might break if I was not careful. The weapon was something from Earth Central. It is one of the reasons Separatists cannot be tolerated because the fragmentation of human civilization greatly increases the possibility of war and war is unthinkable. The cyborg shot back into the sky with the air seeming to distort around it, then it exploded like a balloon filled with hydrogen. I heard the clang and rattle of a few pieces of metal hitting the ground and was turning away before the burning fragments did so. Dragon: answers.

The storm had ceased moments after I killed the cyborg. The black thing had been controlled by one of the many battle programmes in his enlarged skull. I stepped over what was left of Dawn Keltree and walked towards the three cobra heads.

'Dragon!'

As one the three heads turned towards me.

'I want answers from you!'

Even as I said it a part of myself looked on with a cold assurance: how human, how emotional. The three heads curved over me – three great question marks of flesh.

'Answers?' came the distant hiss of a voice. Just then Bird came in from the side, a silver flash, and three giant severed heads thudded to the ground like grain sacks. The hiss became a scream as the three pseudopodia retreated into the ground spattering all around the milky fluid that was Dragon's blood here. Those raw ends broke the surface once, twice, giving me an indication of the direction I must go. I followed, not stopping to wonder if I was meant to. Bird was back at my shoulder: my hawk, we hunted.

Wilderness, broken rock. As I walked following disturbed ground and occasional pools of Dragon blood I admitted to myself that yes answers were important, but that the satisfaction of violence had its place. I looked at the weapon I held and it did not fade from my hand this time. I opened my hand and it stayed affixed to my palm even when I turned it to the ground. This was a weapon that could hurt Dragon, as was Bird, and I wanted to cause hurt. I did not know the extent of Dragon's involvement with the cyborg. What kind of deal had there been? Was Dragon only observing in its coldly alien way? In the end this did not matter to me. All I knew was that Dragon had allowed this. This was Dragon's world. Even if it was only alien indifference Dragon could be blamed for ... I swore as I walked. Whatever. A girl I had quite liked lay in the dirt with her back blown out.

Four conjoined spheres rose over the horizon like a queue of moons, misty at first then clearing. I trudged on and drew closer, and closer still, then, in a state of near delirious exhaustion I stood peering into the shadow and darkness under the first of the spheres.

'You want answers?' hissed the darkness.

'Not particularly,' I said. I pointed the gun in front of me and pulled back on the trigger. The gun collapsed in my hand like burnt paper.

'Here are answers.'

Even Bird did not move fast enough. A great saliva drooling head shot out of the undershadows, two sapphire eyes fixed on me. The jaws closed on me just as Bird shot at the head. I hit the ground and saw the head, severed away, holding the legs and greater part of a human torso in its jaws. I died before I realised it was mine.

I sat on a flat rock in the Dragon shadows and felt regret for my actions. Dragon, another head now drawing away, had been an impartial observer. The cyborg had come by ship so no one was to blame for his actions but himself and the agent who had informed him of my presence on this world, and she lay dead, killed by an employer who had not known who she was. Blegg had been right about some things and wrong about others. He had warned me at the first that Dragon's answer might be death. It was, and though I did not realise it, it was the answer I had then been seeking. So much has been restored.

    Blegg believed Bird was an extension of me. Here he was wrong. I am an extension of Bird, a tool she uses, a program she is allowing to run, only slightly altered for the study of this particular civilization. There have been others. So why does Bird protect me? She protects me because of the work involved in restoring me. There is no altruism or loyalty involved. On this restoration, as on every other one, the memories she had selectively erased, because of their impairment to my function, were returned to me from the master copy. Not fifty years, not three hundred years, and not the millennia I had momentarily glimpsed, and not just one death. These last few centuries with Blegg have been entertaining as he has time and time again led me into situations whereby he might learn something about me, about Bird. Perhaps someday he will know.

    I must now forget.

THE END

Made in United States
North Haven, CT
27 April 2025